Storylandia

The Wapshott Journal of Fiction

Issue 6

Storylandia, Issue 6, The Wapshott Journal of Fiction, ISSN 1947-5349, ISBN 978-0-9825813-7-7, is published at intervals by the Wapshott Press, PO Box 31513, Los Angeles, California, 90031-0513, telephone 323-201-7147. All correspondence can be sent The Wapshott Press, PO Box 31513, LA CA 90031-0513. Visit our website at www.WapshottPress.com This work is copyright © 2012 by Storylandia. The Wapshott Journal of Fiction, Los Angeles, California. Copyrights for the individual stories and cover are held by their respective authors and artist and are reprinted here with the author/artist's permission.

Many thanks to Kathleen Warner and Deana Swart for the proofreads and editorial support.

Storylandia is always seeking quality original short fiction. Please have a look at our submission guidelines at www.Storylandia.WapshottPress.com or email the editor at editor@wapshottpress.com

"Expecting a Star" originally appeared in Golden Visions, 2009.

"The Furtive Men Perform Nightly at the Wretched Street Bar," originally appeared in The Miraculous Hand and Other Stories, 1991.

Cover: "La Quinta," by Magda Audifred, www.magdaaudifred.com

Storylandia

The Wapshott Journal of Fiction

Founded in 2009

Issue 6, Spring 2012

Edited by Ginger Mayerson

Table of Contents

The Deepest Crease Visible 　Paullette Gaudet	1
Amie and Sherry and the Twilight Diner 　Tom Sheehan	17
Expecting a Star 　V. Ulea	32
The Furtive Men Perform Nightly 　at the Wretched Street Bar 　J.J. Steinfeld	38
Best Head Ever 　Dustin Grayson	53
The Mall in Rainbows 　Chris Castle	91

Paullette Gaudet

The Deepest Crease Visible

We were driving back to the city from Indio after the Coachella concert, and Mark, my best friend and roommate, was asking his usual road-trip questions. They had advanced over the years from things like "Would you rather be burned to death, or suffocate?" or "You and boyfriend Quentin Tarantino seek a third, available weekends—who responds to your ad?" to ones like "Would you be willing to live without love, if it meant you could own a house outright?" Mark had adjusted his questions recently to accommodate my increasing retreat from whimsy, I think—his more absurd proposals were now reserved for new acquaintances, and when I overheard them they made me sad for a time when I was younger, and drunker, and still thought I would someday meet Quentin Tarantino. Mark couldn't, even for me, make his questions *completely* dull, so it didn't surprise me when he asked, "Would you ever date a midget?"

I adjusted the pinch of my bra strap and caught a whiff of salt from my tank top, which had only just that morning smelled cheerfully of fabric softener. "It would depend," I said.

Mark shook his head. "There's no depend—yes, or no?" He was looking at the road, driving and scratching his nose. Mark was my gay best friend before there even *were* gay best friends, when you simply spent most of your waking hours together in a puzzling haze of mutual, sexual disinterest. We had known each other for the best part of our lives, as we constantly told ourselves, while just as constantly denying that the best part of our lives might have been fifteen years ago. But back to the midget question.

"Maybe," I said. "But probably not."

Mark rolled his eyes. "Okay, an amputee. Would you date one, or not?"

"I'd have to know him first."

"There's no knowing—just yes, or no!"

I sighed. "If I knew him *before* the amputation, there would be no problem. If I met him *after* the amputation—probably not."

Mark leered at me. "So you're an amputee-cist."

"*No!* Okay, what limb's been cut off?"

"Leg. No, arm," Mark said.

"Well, which is it?"

"*Both*, leg and arm, he was in a war. He's really cute, though."

"Has he read *Gravity's Rainbow*?" I asked.

Mark rolled his eyes again. "*Nobody's* read *Gravity's Rainbow*—he's just a dude, without a leg or an arm."

I sighed again. "No, wouldn't date him."

"Would you date someone six inches shorter than you?" Mark asked.

"I'm five-feet tall—anyone shorter than me is in midget territory, which is a *no*."

"Okay. So you're open to anyone who's not shorter than you, or missing legs or arms. But who would you really, like, *never* date?"

I looked out into the darkness. It was well after midnight, and we had just passed Joshua Tree National Park, and the Morongo casino, which rose twenty-seven stories above miles of windmills. I was tired, from two, ninety-five degree days spent sipping from carefully rationed four-dollar bottles of water. The smuggled smoke of marijuana pipes all around us had perhaps taken hold of me, because I considered Mark's question with more than my usual patronizing glibness.

People often asked what my "type" was, but I could never answer that question because my Ideal Man didn't have a face. Or even a body, really. Just a set of clothes. I saw him as a series of fashion sketches, if you must know. There was one, with university tweeds and corduroys; and another, with dusty Levi's and scuffed work boots. In my favorite sketch, he wore a very European ensemble I saw on Jude Law when he was on *The Today Show* a few months ago—I can't remember the specifics, so blinded was I by the outfit's effortless perfection. I just remember orange leather sneakers, jeans with a fit rarely seen in reality, and a sweater that just...*hung*. Fabulously. To me, clothes weren't simply clothes, they were personalities made visible. And I would just *know*, by someone's clothes, if they were for me.

"I wouldn't date a nudist," I said, finally. "I just couldn't get around that."

Mark smirked. "I guess you're lucky they're easy to spot."

I shook my head. "No, see, you wouldn't know, that's what's so scary. That'd be something that came up around the third time you slept together, that's when all that stuff comes out. The first couple of times are always pretty vanilla, then you go over to his place and he opens the door and brings out a goat and says, 'I thought we could try something a little different tonight'."

Mark chuckled. "That only happened to me once, and we said we'd never speak of it again."

I punched his shoulder. "Shut up! I'm serious!"

"Okay, okay! So you wouldn't date a nudist."

"Ever," I added. And I meant it, really, at the time.

A month after Coachella, the Los Angeles sky was finally visible through a break in the early "June Gloom." I was sitting in a juice bar and waiting for a man to take me to Malibu for the weekend, which were two—no, *three*—things I never thought I'd do, in a place that wasn't yet my home.

I had met Julian in a crush of new people at a tiny Los Feliz bar, one so crowded that I couldn't even see what he was wearing. I had only stayed in hotels with Julian, since he was apparently a businessman of some sort who practically lived in hotel rooms. My favorite was the Downtown Standard hotel, with its glass-walled showers, and fancy room service breakfast cards that asked: "Watermelon juice, or carrot? Please check which." It was news to me that Julian owned a house near Malibu, and not welcome news, at that. I had just gotten used to being Hotel Girl, and him being Businessman Guy, and us being...well, kind of perfect for each other. I thought Malibu might ruin that—might ruin everything, with questions of what to stock in the refrigerator, and who would load the dishwasher. It was too many things to consider, too soon...but Julian had dimples, and consistently filed fingernails, and had never once asked me for money.

"I don't know about Malibu," I had told him last week, honestly.

He looked down at his perfect nails. "I finished *Gravity's Rainbow* on my trip to Tokyo. What the fuck was that?"

I smiled—Thomas Pynchon was my *final* final test; I'd had to create a new one after Julian had sat, completely alert, through all six hours of Matthew Barney's *Cremaster Cycle*. "Okay," I said. "I'll go to Malibu. Pick me up after work on Friday."

So now it was Friday, and Julian came in, and kissed me—I tightened the lid on my juice drink and got into his car, which was shiny and didn't have a top. We drove quickly on one of those freeways Los Angelinos always preface with "*the*": *the* 90, *the* 5, *the* 10. I didn't know which one we were on, only that it was next to the ocean and the sun was setting, and even though my feet were braced hard against the floorboards, I was skidding just as hard into love with the man next to me, who shifted gears and smiled into the wind as we tore past two shirtless men with surfboards on the side of the road.

We arrived at Julian's gated community and drove to a twinkling house on a bluff, a modern Spanish mini-mansion with white Christmas lights on every shrub and arch, the fairytale castle most modern women would kill themselves before admitting they longed to enter—well, at least *I* would, or thought I would, but instead I flung my seat belt out of the way so I could jump out of the car and run to the house's front door.

After food and sex—both in the infinity pool—I sat on a pillow-topped mattress and thought that it wouldn't matter so much if I fell asleep and never woke up—on Pratesi sheets, I could pretty much die happy.

The next morning I put on my peach silk robe and walked downstairs to the large, Mexican-tiled kitchen. Julian—nude—was blending something in the blender. He turned and handed me a glass of frothy, violet-colored juice. "I made watermelon-carrot smoothies, so you don't have to choose, like at the Standard." Then he unfastened my sash and said, "You don't need your robe—c'mon, let's go outside."

We sat in the back garden, naked on puffy, water-repellent cushions. Bushes and flowers framed a view of ridiculously blue water that stretched, without impediment, to Hawaii, or maybe even Tokyo. I sipped my smoothie as a nude, older couple opened the gate to his backyard garden, and approached us with smiles and waves. "*Hellooo*, Julian," trilled the woman, as the man refastened the latch on the gate.

"Marnie! Good morning!" Julian said. He embraced her, nude, and kissed her cheeks, then shook the hand of her companion. "Bernard, it's good to see you. Let me introduce you to Bella."

I was frozen at this point, looking up at the trio of naked people before me. "Hello?" I said.

"Hello, dear, we're so glad to meet you," said Marnie.

"Mornin'," said Bernard.

"Come on in, let me get you a smoothie," Julian said.

I watched, as they walked into the kitchen. Nude.

I sat, and thought about my childhood, spent pleasantly enough in small houses with decently manicured lawns. No one had ever been nude, that I remembered. I rarely saw anyone nude, even now as an adult. I didn't know what to do, but then knew who would: Mark.

I padded through the open sliding-glass door and went upstairs, unseen by those in the kitchen. In the master bedroom I fished in my purse for my cell phone and looked out at the cul-de-sac below, where similar Spanish mini-mansions primly sat with sprinklers spraying and naked men edging their lawns. I pressed closer to the window and saw they were *everywhere:* waxing Mercedes-Benz's, trimming hedges and waving to each other—middle-aged men wearing baseball caps and sneakers and nothing else.

I pressed "one" on my speed-dial, still looking outside, and Mark eventually answered. "What the fuck are you doing calling me this early on a Saturday?" he growled.

"They're naked, Mark, all of them," I whispered. "I'm in naked-Stepford and they're *naked*."

"What are you talking about?" asked Mark, still sounding groggy.

"I'm in Malibu, surrounded by naked people. How much clearer do I have to be?!"

I heard the distinct click of a cigarette lighter on Mark's end. "So," he said, "I'm assuming this isn't a *good* everyone's-naked thing."

"No, it's not. I am apparently in an upscale nudist gated community, with my boyfriend who is apparently a nudist, and with two elderly nudist neighbors downstairs sipping smoothies while nude," I hissed.

"Yeah, that was kind of implied. Didn't you see all the naked people when you got there?"

"It was dark! It was late. There were white Christmas lights everywhere."

"Hey—does Julian have an infinity pool?" asked Mark.

"Yes. Look, I don't have a lot of time—what do I do?"

I could actually hear Mark shrug, because his shoulder pushed the phone against his cheek. "I would say be cool and go with it. Look, Julian obviously thought you would be okay with this or else he would have said something beforehand, right?"

I didn't know, and said so. "How could he possibly think I would be cool with this? How could he not warn me?"

"Well, maybe this is *his* 'Cremaster Cycle'," Mark said.

I hung up on him and did not call back.

I had to go back downstairs—I couldn't just stay up in the master bedroom holding my silent cell phone. Or could I...no, I had to go downstairs, and soon.

"*There* you are!" said Marnie. She and the others were huddled in front of the blender.

"What's on the agenda for you guys today?" Julian asked.

"I have to return a rake at the hardware store," said Marnie. "Can you believe that something costing forty-five dollars would just fall apart the first time you used it?"

Bernard snorted. "*I* can—everything's made with

crap and spit, these days."

Marnie blushed, and looked down at the tiled floor. "I have to admit I've been avoiding going into town for a while now, because…well, *you* know."

Everyone else nodded.

"Because what?" I asked, raising an eyebrow in the kitchen's ever-expanding silence.

"Textiles!" Bernard finally barked.

My eyebrow stayed where it was. Julian kept cleaning his blender, but Marnie put an arm around my shoulders, her hand icy from its recent grip on her smoothie. "*People who insist on wearing clothes*," she whispered.

"Oh," I said, nodding knowingly. "*Them.*"

Julian wiped his hands with a dish towel. "You're still coming to dinner tonight?"

"Of course, we're looking forward to it!" said Marnie. She hugged me before leaving, while a handshake sufficed for Bernard.

The kitchen, empty now, was quiet enough to hear the crash of waves below. I felt, for perhaps the first time in my life, that this was an actual moment of *choice*. I usually hated that word, especially when used by Dr. Phil or others on pseudo-psychological rants:

"That was your *choice*."

"You *chose* to do that."

Mark, in particular, was fond of saying, "You *choose* the wrong men," as if ten eligible guys were constantly lined up before me and each time I willfully selected the alcoholic ex-convict. It's not like that, I would insist—there's just nothing, for a long time, until suddenly there's the glimmer of something, so you pursue it. Choice, to me, meant you got to see all of your options before making a decision, and that had never been the case. Now, though, I saw that whatever I said next was going to completely change everything that happened afterward. I saw this, and I *chose*—I chose to be cool.

"What are we serving for dinner?" I asked.

Julian smiled, but I couldn't tell if it was with relief. "We have some time to decide that. Let's go to the beach."

I wish I could say that no one was playing volleyball on the beach. I really do. But, I can't. I kept thinking that if *I* were a nudist, I would never play volleyball, even if I loved it, just to avoid the cliché. And then I started wondering why it was a cliché—nude volleyball, and tennis and ping-pong. I finally figured out that the attraction must be the net—you need a dividing line between teams when you can't do shirts and skins. Julian and I sat on beach towels and watched his neighbors play. They were young, but Julian was reading an old *US Weekly* and didn't seem to notice the parade of supple, bronzed flesh before him. I did, though.

"Do all of these people live next to you?" I asked.

Julian glanced up, then back at his magazine. "Most of my neighbors are older, since it's pretty expensive to live here, but they have college-aged kids who come up."

"They're definitely attractive," I said. "And naked."

Julian shrugged. "Nudity is the body's natural state, no matter what condition that body is in. It's all just...*meat*."

I asked, "They're what—nineteen, twenty? Did

they grow up as nudists, or is this just something they do to please their parents when they're home?"

"A lot of people come to nudism later in life. I don't know how families address the issue," said Julian. "I've really never thought about it."

I'd never thought about it, either, but now I couldn't think of anything else. Except maybe dinner—I was starting to get hungry.

Later, when rows of neatly-skewered shrimp were lined up on cookie sheets and covered with plastic wrap in the fridge, I asked Julian if we were dressing for dinner.

"Oh, yes, I should have said something, it's going to be a little swanky. I'd say a necklace and earrings, if you have them, and some nice heels."

"So people are going to be wearing jewelry?" I asked.

"Oh, yeah—jewelry, shoes, purses. We're not *barbarians*," Julian said.

I almost rolled my eyes, but stopped myself. "I have a necklace," I said. I almost added, *to go with the dress I brought with me.*

Julian nodded. "That's fine. People here aren't all that material. I mean, they like their shoes and all, but it's really not important." He paused. "It'll be great. Just be yourself."

"Okay," I said. "I guess I'll go...change."

Julian's doorbell featured a brief cascade of tinkly notes that formed the chorus of "Fly Me To the Moon," just like Jennifer the receptionist's apartment doorbell on *WKRP in Cincinnati*. The doorbell rang three times, to announce Marnie and Bernard and two other middle-aged couples.

I recorded everything in my mind, to tell Mark later. All of the couples were nude, except for expensive jewelry and shoes. There were no coats to take, so we were all soon gathered in the living room. I sat down on a plush couch next to a framed photograph of an older naked couple I assumed were Julian's parents—they sat smiling in a backyard, the woman's breasts resting in her lap while the man's testicles plunged in a sad, sorry race to the ground through the plastic slats of a lawn chair.

"How was everyone's day?" asked Julian, entering the room with his drink. My gaze fell to his now-perky crotch, and lingered there in speculation of its future.

Tania Tillman, a short woman with sassy hair, said, "I trimmed my rosebushes. And, my granddaughter called."

"How's she doing?" Lynda Sargent asked. She succeeded, after two tries, in crossing her thick legs.

"Oh, she's busy with classes, and needs money, of course," Tania said. The rest of the guests laughed loudly.

Bill Sargent, a trim man covered in frizzy gray body hair, snorted. "If they only knew what shit they'll have to put up with after graduation."

I sat, smiling, and clutched a sofa pillow to my chest as Bernard complained that someone named Tormund was apparently not edging his lawn to community specifications, while Marnie urged leniency based on Tormund's upcoming divorce—of *course* he had other things on his mind than his lawn. I gradually tuned out the chitchat, and wondered how we had all gotten here—a bunch of near-strangers sitting naked together. I wanted to ask them if they had ever not been nudists, and what they would think if they knew that a textile was in their midst.

"Dinner's ready!" Julian called, and we all moved to the dining room.

The dining room was really, truly beautiful—there were mirrors and crystal, and a sparkly chandelier. It was still somehow odd to see a bunch of naked, bejeweled older people sitting down at a glass dining table set with white flowers, but no one except me seemed to think it was strange. I had thought that if I could just get through this night, I would be okay with any number of similar nights in the future. Until today, I had never really thought of having children, but I suddenly had visions of little children-people who looked like me, and I didn't want them to know what their parents looked like naked. I don't really even know why I did it, but I stood up. "Excuse me," I said.

Four naked men rose to acknowledge my departure from the table. I walked upstairs and put on the Cynthia Rowley party dress from my overnight bag, then went back downstairs.

Marnie shook her head when I entered the dining room. "Oh, *Bella*."

"I knew it," Bernard said.

Tania Tillman cleared her throat. "Um, we were just talking about...I'm sorry, dear, but what are you wearing?"

"Cynthia Rowley," I said.

"I mean...it's a dress," Tania said.

Her husband raised his hand. "Look, we're all reasonable people here–"

Tania shook her head and pointed a finger at Julian. "You're dating a *textile*?"

Julian coughed. "I didn't know she would... I don't see how...um, Marnie?"

"I'm concerned, Julian," Marnie said. "You would think that a houseguest—and *girlfriend*, I presume—would be able to assimilate for a weekend."

Julian coughed again. "Well, we really didn't discuss things before I invited Bella here. She's been very accommodating, as I hope you all will be-"

"I cannot believe you expected me to eat dinner with a textile!" said Tania. She turned to the table for support. "What should we do, Lynda—put on robes, or pantsuits?" Lynda opened her mouth, but then shut it in the face of Tania's fury.

Luckily, there were no coats to search for—Julian's guests simply stood up, and left. Someone accidentally pressed against the doorbell while leaving, and the chimes of "Fly Me to the Moon" echoed throughout the empty house.

Julian's forehead, usually so smooth, now formed creases deeper than I'd thought imaginable. He shook his head. "They—and *I*—feel that nudity is our natural state. I thought I'd been clear about that."

"*When*?" I said. "When were you clear about that?"

"At the Standard, a couple weeks ago," said Julian. "It was—what, the third time we'd spent the night together. I was walking around naked and you said to put some clothes on, and I said this was my home away from home so I didn't have to. I completely remember saying, 'This is what I do, at home and in my community'."

I stared at him as my memory came crashing back. "You did say that."

"What did you think I meant?" said Julian.

"Not this! Not naked people everywhere and me being naked with them!" I said.

"I don't see the problem," said Julian. "My neighbors are all just people, what does it matter that they're not wearing clothes?"

He was right, really; Marnie and Bernard had been perfectly delightful over smoothies that morning—well, *Marnie* had, at least—and the others were nice as well, until they shunned me. They were people with jobs, families, and home appliances—who was *I* to insist they wear clothes?

Of course, I knew this was about me, and not Julian's neighbors. "I can't raise a bunch of naked children, while naked."

"What?" said Julian.

"I'm sorry," I said, "I can't...do this. For the rest of my life." And then I called a very expensive taxi.

Later that night, in Silver Lake, I drank vodka-cranberries at a bar with Mark. "So that was it?" he asked. "You just left?"

I tilted my head, and sipped my drink. "What else was there to say? He's a nudist, I'm not. It isn't exactly something you can work around."

"I could totally be a nudist on weekends," Mark said.

I shook my head. "See, you say that, but let me tell you again about the drapey skin, and—well, there's the lawn maintenance, for one thing."

Mark drained his drink, and motioned for another round. "Yeah, but you really seemed to like this guy."

I sucked watery vodka from the base of my glass before relinquishing it to the bartender. "*You* didn't."

"I never like anybody you date," Mark said. "I rarely like anybody *I* date."

I tried to spin around on my barstool, but it only clicked a couple of degrees in either direction. "Then who? Fucking who is it I'm supposed to be with, Mark—am I just supposed to sit in bars talking about my last horrible boyfriend for the rest of my life?"

"Jesus fuck, simmer down," Mark said.

"I'm serious! This guy might have led to something," I said.

Mark rolled his eyes. "How many times have you ended up on a barstool next to me?"

I paused, because he was right, the fucker. This was what we did, console each other after each three-week or three-month relationship; what we would do, apparently, forever. I sipped my drink as an old song came up on the jukebox, one from fifteen years ago.

Mark smiled. "Wanna dance?"

"Yeah," I said. "I do."

But we both, as usual, stayed on our barstools and watched everyone else instead.

Tom Sheehan

Amie and Sherry and the Twilight Diner

On the morning of her 25th birthday, on a July day, Amie Lightstreet walked into the Twilight Diner, just off Exit 185, US 80 eastbound, in Pennsylvania. She went immediately to a table in the far corner, the last empty booth in the diner just before a couple came in the door. The waitress hurried over with a menu and said, "Coffee, Hon?"

The waitress's name was Sherry, just starting to get round and she noticed how slim her new customer was, and how beautiful, the way she once was and hoped she held to some of it. She thought the girl was looking for someone.

"I would love a cup of tea, if it's no bother this early in the day." Her voice was sweet, her eyes were startlingly blue, and her clothes were a smooth combination of white and tan.

"You got it, Hon. You looking for someone special?"

"Aren't we all looking for someone special?" Amie Lightstreet had a great smile that warmed Sherry in the midst of the morning rush.

"Unless we got him already," Sherry said. Over her shoulder as she walked off to get the tea, she added, "Mine's name is Josh. Good luck on yours."

Amie had breakfast, dawdling over her food. She had a second cup of tea, and with every sip looked at the door if it was opened and then out the window.

Sherry, looking at the clock as it neared 11 AM, hoped whoever the girl in the corner booth was looking for would come in before her shift was done. She wanted to feel that stab of goodness that now and then ran right through her. All customers had left but the girl in the corner and an elderly couple in another booth. The traffic outside, had thinned out to a standstill. A light mist began to fall. The elderly male customer went to his car and brought back an umbrella.

Sherry said to the girl in the corner booth, "Doesn't that take all. I hope we both come to that. They look so sweet, the two old timers."

Amie said, "Don't we all have a grandmother or grandfather story." It was not a question. She looked at the door as another young couple walked in.

Sherry said, "We sure do. I got mine." She turned to the grill as the burly gent in an apron said, "Sherry, go on and git now. I got breakfast for you and Josh and the boys all wrapped up for you. See you in the morning. I'll get that new couple."

The next morning, at about 9:30, Amie Lightstreet came into the Twilight Diner, looked around, and again found the corner booth available. This time, after a small delay with other customers being served, Sherry brought her a cup of tea. "I'm Sherry, and I hope Mr. Whoever shows up for you today."

Amie, feeling the pleasant acceptance from Sherry, said, "My name is Amie. I remember you saying yesterday that you had a grandmother story. I'd like to hear it sometime."

Sherry, checking out her landscape, letting the clock work in her head about customers' servings, said, "I have a beauty, but it'll take time to tell. If you're around as long as yesterday, I'll tell you. You live near here?"

Amie said, "Oh, it's about 7 or 8 miles away. It's a nice ride."

"There's got to be a few other diners between here and there."

Amie cranked out that gorgeous smile again, and Sherry could almost reach back to touch her own youthful smile, the one that had crushed Josh. Amie said, "I bet you'd agree with me that there's only one Twilight Diner."

She looked quickly at the entrance as the door swung inward. Two burly truckers walked in and sat at the counter. The man behind the grill greeted them by name. They leaned over and there was a minute three-man convention and then all three broke into hearty laughter.

Sherry said to Amie, "It's the joke of the day for Mike and the boys. Kind of like their own email JOD. They used to play ball together years ago." The summation came on her face before she said, "They're nice guys. The good kind."

Suddenly, with a serious look on her face, Amie said, "Does happiness come with this place?"

Behind the grill, Mike yelled, "#2 and 3 up, Sherry." He and his pals still had wide morning grins. One of them was still chuckling.

Traffic inside and out came and went and the morning ebb had begun. The sun was slanting steeply into the windows and touching the floor. Shadows of tables and booths became shorter. Sizzling bacon sounds had disappeared but the aroma held place in the air. A long semi, with a galloping horse logo spread along the side of the trailer, ground to a halt along the roadside. Two cars of customers left the diner. Amie Lightstreet sat in the same booth with the same expectant attitude breathing about her that Sherry swore she could measure.

The good thoughts came back as she remembered Amie saying, "Does happiness come with this place?" In the back of her mind a thin dark piece of matter reached out to touch her consciousness. She could feel a literal connection had been made. The image of her grandmother rushed through her and she remembered her promise to Amie, at that moment looking hopefully as the door opened. A young couple walked in and Sherry could tell the girl was embarrassed that the boy was holding her hand. He would not let go, as if he was telling her something. Sherry smiled at both of them. "Kids," she said to herself, and smiled again as her promise came back.

The clock said 10:55 and Mike held up Sherry's breakfast doggie bag. She said, "I'm going to sit with Amie for a while, Mike. I told Josh I'd be late with his breakfast." She waited on the new customers, the only others beside Amie in the Twilight Diner. She put her carry-out on Amie's table and sat down with a cup of coffee. "You want another tea, Hon?" The sudden lack of motion created a sense of suspense in the diner, as Mike behind the counter had gone into a back room, and the young couple was silent, only eyes working. Both Amie and Sherry were aware of the change.

"No, I'm set," Amie said, "but I'd love to hear that grandmother story of yours."

"Only if you tell me yours," Sherry said, "and it's not too long."

"Oh, I'll be here again tomorrow. I think I'll be here every day until I leave town in September. I'll be going to Chicago."

The whole story flashed through Sherry's mind and said so on her face. Amie could read the happiness and the pain that must have been riding through her new friend. She saw both the hurt and the good times take turns on Sherry's face, and finally a happy grin took over. Amie made up her mind that it would all end up as a happy story.

Sherry said, "I was almost as pretty as you as a kid. I'm 31 now and have three kids. Young Josh is almost 16, McKenzie is 13, a girl, and my baby Cavan is 9. My husband's name is Josh and I have been in love with him since I was 12 or 13 and he was a neighbor. When he was a big football hero for the high school and I was a cheerleader and had all the equipment in the right places, he knew I liked him and someone told me he liked me. Anyway, one night we ended up in the back seat of his father's car and he's so nice and dumb I have to get my bra off for him. Oh, he was so clumsy and nervous, but so damned nice. Can you imagine a great big football player who could run like the devil was chasing him, having trouble with my bra? Anyway, I said what the hell and took my panties off for him too, and he was mesmerized. I loved that because every time until then that I had touched myself, it was for him. Every single time for a few years. So, you know what happened. I got pregnant and he refused to go off to college. He had a chance to go to Penn State. Uncle Joe had even come to see one of his games. But Josh wanted his child to be his child, not some other guy's. We got married right after my 16th birthday and after he graduated and went right to work. He wouldn't take anything from his father, who had two other sons."

Sherry looked at the clock again, and continued. "I keep looking at the clock because I don't like to be too late. Josh is in a wheelchair now, but he takes care of the kids in his way and I'm in here at 5 in the morning helping Mike who loves me like I'm his kid sister."

"What happened with Josh?" Amie's face was gathered into a grimace of pain.

"Well, times were tough, and he worked a couple of jobs. He learned how to use tools from his father, so he did a lot of different kinds of jobs. And he joined the Army reserves to get some extra money. You know what happened then? He went off to Iraq and they kicked the crap out of him and he came home in a wheelchair and things were real tough, but my grandmother stepped in. This is the nice part of my grandmother story; she was widowed and had an old house with four bedrooms and she told Josh and me we could move in and we'd have the house after she died. She was a sweetheart, let me tell you. Never went out with a single guy after my grandfather died in a car crash. Her name was Mathie Brown without an *e*, but I'll tell you about that later."

"So Josh finally relented and took something from somebody. He was never sorry for himself. Never cried once. Some of the good parts are coming back for him now, because young Josh promises to be even better as a football player than his father. Anyway, he relented and said we'd take my grandmother's offer, but there was a problem. There was no ramp to get him in or out, but his father, who is a widower, and his older brother, who is a school assistant principal but handy with tools, came to my grandmother and said they'd build a ramp for Josh, but there was another problem. The front porch was in such bad shape, they'd have to make it to the back door, but they promised they'd eventually build one out front."

"They built the back ramp and we moved in, and then Josh's father went to my grandmother and said, Mrs. Brown, I'd like to build a new porch out front but at no cost to you. We'll always keep out of your way, as much as we can. Jeff and I will do the work and some friends, who remember how well Josh could run, have promised supplies, either new or used, to get it done. She said to go ahead. They were relentless. They came every weekend, like they were driven to atone for something. But I was wrong there; it was out of love. They were special people. They made Josh what he was and is, me and my kids being the lucky ones. They built a new porch out front, with a special ramp, and it was like they wanted to tie the one out front to the one out back, and they went right through the house on all those weekends. They put new stairs up from the front hall, and a new railing, and then a new front hall floor, and they put up new cabinets in the kitchen, and new windows in every room and new doors. They worked there, usually the two of them, and sometimes just Josh's dad when Jeff was off with his wife and kids or on some school thing."

Amie was smiling and happiness bubbled on her face, and Sherry knew its warmth.

"My name now is Sherry Browne with an *e*. It used to be Sherry Brown without an *e*. So, almost two years after they started working on the house, with all that time around us, and the kids loving their grandmother and grandfather, Josh's dad said to my grandmother one day, "Mrs. Brown, why don't you put an *e* on the end of your name and come live with me in my house. We'll leave this one to the kids and you'll have mine if I pass on before you. And she smiled at him, after all that time of being alone, and then being around him, and said, "Mr. Browne, I would love to do that."

Sherry, who had tears in the corners of her eyes, could see that Amie was really sharing her grandmother story. She patted Amie on her arm and said, "I've talked too long, Amie. I've got to run. See you tomorrow?"

"I'll be here."

For three days, Amie did not show up. Sherry felt the loss and wondered, knowing that Amie was looking for something special, if she had been driven off by her story. Mike noticed the change in Sherry's attitude. "Something bothering you, Sherry? Looks like you lost a pal."

"You know what that girl said to me, that Amie who sat in the corner booth, 'Does happiness come with this place?'"

Mike nodded, his bald head catching some of the overhead light, softness still managing to display itself around him. "Hey, kid, we ain't done bad here. Neither one of us will be a millionaire, but we'll get by. You're a damned good worker and I couldn't have done it without you and I know you never lifted a buck from me, and I've had a few who did just that."

"You're an old softie, Mike."

"That makes us the odd pair, kid. It's a pleasure to know you."

At that moment the door opened and Amie, sad in the face, came into the diner. She sat in her usual place.

For the first time in the Twilight Diner, Sherry was afraid to approach a customer. She stood back, looking at Amie who finally looked up and motioned her over.

"I had some bad news. I lost my grandmother. She'd been ill, and I had to be with my mother, but I kept thinking about your story and knew I had to tell you mine, but whenever you're ready."

"Oh, Hon, I told Josh every day I might be a bit late, thinking you'd be coming in. You just sit here and wait until I get finished. I'll get your tea."

She walked off lighter on her feet than she had been in three days. Mike saw the change immediately and nodded, then saw his two old teammates walk in the door and the Twilight Diner was back in motion.

Sherry finally sat with Amie in the corner booth. "I'm sorry for your loss, Amie. I was thinking about you. How's everything else?" Each of them understood she meant the reason for Amie's vigilance at the Twilight Diner.

At length, with another look at the door and new customers entering, two middle-aged women, Amie said, "My grandmother told me this story a thousand times. She told me to the very last day, almost whispering at the end to my mother and me, not sure who was there or who was listening, "Tell Amie his name is Travis. His grandmother said he'd come. I know he will."

"Who's Travis?" Sherry said. "Is that Mr. Special?"

Amie nodded and said, "You may not believe this story, now what I have made of it, but it has taken hold of my life."

"I have all morning, Hon," Sherry said, and put her elbows on the table and set her eyes on Amie's eyes.

"It began right here," Amie said, and she pointed at the one large table near her booth that could seat six people. "Right at that table, or one just like it, and all of twenty years ago."

The sun was now at their feet and touching them lightly. Amie's tea was tepid and Sherry's coffee mug was empty. The diner was silent. Mike was off behind the counter someplace.

"My grandmother, my mother, my two sisters and I were in here having breakfast. I was five years old. Sara was eight and Grace was eleven. An older couple came in. My grandmother said she liked them right off as they toasted each other with their coffee cups, and remembers both had black coffee, as if she was trying to remember every detail. The woman was thin and wore glasses and had a nice smile. The man was a little heavy around the belly and wore a baseball cap with the name of a hockey team on it, so it must have been a hockey cap. Grandma said I had bangs just like her and that I was a beautiful child and this older couple kept looking over at us. And finally the man said, 'The children are very well behaved and very beautiful, all of them.' Grandma said she almost busted loose, it made her feel so good. She said she felt all this goodness pouring through her."

Sherry nodded. "I know that feeling. Do you

really think it's this place? 'Member when you asked me if this place brings happiness?"

"I knew then that I'd have to be telling you my story sometime, because I can use all the help I can get."

"What is it, Hon? Is it a guy? I'm on pins and needles."

"Well, the couple kept looking over at us and smiling, and then they'd go on talking. Grandma said it was like sometimes there was nobody else in the room for them. She kept saying that, and then she'd say they came back from wherever they went and looked back at us. She said the man's cap said Saugus Hockey and he wore a blue Penn State T-shirt and light pants and black sneakers, like she was trying to put every detail in place."

"What about his wife?"

"She wore glasses, wore blue jeans, a blue short sleeve shirt, a gold bracelet, a watch, and had two rings on her fingers. One was a diamond ring."

"So, they were a married couple?"

"Oh, she knew that at first glance. Then they got their bill from the waitress and the woman counted out the money from her pocketbook. They got up to leave, the man letting her go ahead of him. They got right abreast of my grandmother and the woman looked down at me and said to my grandma, 'I have a special grandson whose name is Travis, and someday, about twenty years from now, if he becomes the man I am sure he will become, he will come looking for her,' and she nodded down at me. Grandma said a bolt of something went right through her and I have felt that same thing most of my life, each and every time she tells the story. I bet she has told it a thousand times, like she's been foretelling my future every time she does so."

"Oh, Amie. That's a beautiful story. I'll pray he walks in here today or tomorrow. Oh, yes."

Amie was true to her grandmother. She came every day, and the two women talked and Amie heard about young Josh doing well at practice and his father able to watch him and his grandfather and new grandmother sitting in a car at the other end of the field and able to pick out Josh's every move on the field.

Sherry told her about the other kids and Amie told Sherry about her sisters and how things were with them, and the summer advanced and late August dumped down on the Twilight Diner as if the evening moon had disappeared.

Amie came in one morning, got her tea, told a story with her face, and said to Sherry, "I'm all packed now, Sherry. Today's my last day. I have to go to Chicago if I want to keep that new position." She looked at the door as it opened and two girls and their father walked in and sat at the counter. She and Sherry shrugged their shoulders.

An hour passed and Amie got fidgety and finally stood up and Sherry came and gave her a hug and said, "If he comes in, I'll tell him you waited almost the whole summer for him." She hugged Amie again.

Amie said, "Tell him I waited twenty years or so and just have someplace else to go." She went out the door and yelled out, "Good luck, Mike. She's a princess, but you know that."

He waved back. "Good luck, Amie."

Her little red car drove out of the diner parking lot and two minutes later a handsome young man walked in the door. He had blond hair and blue eyes and looked like a peach of a kid, and then Sherry almost fainted as she looked at his T-shirt that read, in blue letters, TRAVIS.

(The story was ending here, the way things sometimes go, but I heard another shout, and it kept at me.)

Sherry looked at the clock again and rushed over to him. "Are you looking for someone, like a girl?"

He stared at her. He was not sure what she was saying. "Her name is Amie. Did your grandmother tell you a story?"

His eyes lit up. "For twenty years almost, she told me the same story over and over, about this place."

"She's waited all summer for you. She's on her way to Chicago. She's in a small red car. She's driving straight through, she said."

"I've seen all kinds of little red cars. What kind of a red car?"

"Oh, just red. Just small. She's a beautiful girl. Go after her. Don't lose her. She thinks happiness comes from this little diner. I know it does."

"No idea of what kind of car?"

Sherry ran to the menu board and grabbed a bright red marker. She handed it to Travis. "Her name is Amie. She knows your name is Travis. Your grandmother told your name to her grandmother right here in this room, all those twenty years ago, right there at that table. Write a message on the back window of your car, something she'll see and know. Oh, Travis, chase her, don't miss her. I know she'll love you and you'll love her. Both of you have waited most of your lives for this. Go! Go! Go! Go now!"

She was pushing him and yelling and Mike ran out from behind the counter. Sherry held up her hand. "Hurry, Travis, hurry."

Mike understood in a second and knew that he and Sherry had been part of something special. The two of them watched as Travis ran out and began writing on the back window of a silver-blue minivan. They could not read what he had written as the van buzzed out of the parking lot, swung left and climbed to the westbound side of Route 80, but it said, in bright red letters, "Amie, I'm Travis!!!"

Sherry and Mike carried on their small diner ministry of happiness, as they began to call it, and it was more than a year and a half later, on a lovely April day when Sherry was at home and the children were out back where their grandfather was putting the finishing touches on a gazebo. She was locked into wondering again about Amie, as she did just about every day. All the options, all the chances, all the possibilities had flooded her mind. Josh knew all the scores; every one of them she had recounted so many times.

Sherry saw the car coming down the road leading to their house, the sun flashing off the windshield and the chrome trim. She shook herself out of the swirl of daydreaming that usually grabbed her in off-work hours. Moments later Josh heard her crying and propelled the wheelchair hurriedly into the front room. She was leaning over the front room table where she had been working on a scrapbook and the sobs were rolling out of her.

He yelled, "What's the matter, Hon? What's

wrong?" The wheel chair crashed into her chair.

"Oh, Josh," she said, "I'm so happy I could scream."

He saw the movement out the window. A young girl was bundling up a newborn, a young man was holding the door for her, and Josh knew everything that had come away from the Twilight Diner, where Sherry and happiness happened and hung out together, all as told so long ago.

V. Ulea

Expecting a Star

She was expecting a baby.

"What are you having?" he wondered, watching the sunset.

"I think it's going to be a star," she said quietly, answering his thoughts.

He only smiled, caressing her head. She still looked like a girl—slim and lithe, her shoulders buried in a golden waterfall of hair.

Last time she gave birth to a wave. Emerald green—just like the color of her eyes—and it added music to the ocean.

"The ocean is silent on the inside and sounding on the outside," she had said. "It needs music..." She had not known she was pregnant with the wave.

She was unlike anyone he'd met, and his friends often wondered if their marriage would last long. All of them had stable families. His best friend's wife, for example, gave birth to a vine. It coiled around their house, shading it from the midday heat. It grew quickly, endowing them with numerous other vines and sweet grapes. They always had grapes on their table in addition to a fine wine they learned how to produce.

"One day, you'll also have something like this," his friend had said proudly then. It was almost a light year ago. They had been sitting on the terrace, it was a hot day in July, and the setting sun resembled a mad sunflower from Van Gogh's painting.

His own wife had smiled shyly, leaning against his shoulder.

"Lithia," he whispered into her ear, letting her know that her name was not a secret to him, anymore. Yes, her name was Lithia, it had occurred to him right at that moment, although they had known each other for quite some time.

She had shivered and looked straight into his eyes, their undulating emerald color stunned him. He immediately realized that she was pregnant with something absolutely unique, something none of his friends could've had.

"Do you really think it's going to be a star this time?" he asked, kissing her forehead.

"I'm almost positive."

"How do you know that?"

"It's a feeling."

"What kind of feeling?"

"Everything sparkles inside me…"

"Then it's definitely a star," he said.

"Yes… Just don't tell your mother – she'll be very disappointed. I can't give you anything tangible…" She sighed.

"I won't tell her, don't worry."

"Is it a star?" his mother asked, glancing over Lithia. She appeared out of nowhere, right in the middle of their conversation.

Lithia blushed. She never learned how to hide her

true feelings.

"Why do you make such an assumption, mother?" he asked.

"Why? Are you kidding me? She's shining from within! What else could it be?" She lit a cigarette and inhaled the smoke. "I'm very disappointed in both of you!" She exhaled a cloud and went away.

His mother never came back, but the cloud stayed, suppressing the shine coming from the star ripening in her womb.

"What if it's not a star?" Lithia began to doubt, noticing the decrease of the shine.

"Of course it is!" he tried to console her. "Even my mother said so… Besides, the shine is still there, it's undeniable."

"Well, Lola recently gave birth to a ten karat diamond, you know. She had also shone from within during her pregnancy…"

"It's Lola, not you, baby! You can't possibly give birth to a diamond! It's not in your genes! Genes matter, at this point."

"Still…"

"And even if it is a diamond we'll raise it as a star. The role of family is no less important than genes, you know."

The cloud didn't dissolve.

"If it doesn't go away we won't be able to see when the star is born," Lithia worried.

For the first time he kept quiet. He didn't know what to say simply because he had no experience in a star's birth.

He went to an astronomer to find out more about it.

"We're expecting a star," he told him, "but we have a cloud in the house. Can the cloud affect the birth of the star?"

"What? Are you serious? Do you really expect a star?" The Astronomer put his telescopic glasses on. "Where is she, your wife? Did you bring her for evaluation?"

"No, I didn't. I came here without her knowledge. She's been nervous lately about the cloud... and I decided to consult you because... I have no one else here to talk to."

"You're absolutely right! There's no one here to talk about the birth of the star, but me! Anyway, I must see your wife as soon as possible. Would you take me to her?"

The Astronomer rushed like a comet along the streets, telling a story about his own wife.

"My wife only managed to give birth to a few meteorites, and after artificial insemination at that! Your wife didn't have the artificial insemination, did she?"

"No, she didn't."

"That's good! Then you're the father..."

"Yes, I am." He barely kept pace with the Astronomer.

"What's your name?"

"My name? Uh... I don't know yet. She has not yet told me..."

"Oh! Is that true?" The Astronomer stopped for a

moment, catching his breath. "Then she must be in a hurry! Stars must have their fathers!"

"We were mainly worried about the cloud..."

"The cloud? What cloud? Clouds don't matter! Fathers. Fathers matter!"

She was in bed already when they entered her room. A sphere of stellar rays surrounded her.

"Lithia, this is the Astronomer. He says the cloud will do no harm."

The Astronomer adjusted his telescopic eyeglasses. "She's giving birth tonight," he announced, beaming with excitement. "I can see it clearly. We just need the father's name on the star's birth certificate."

"Lithia, we need my name on the star's birth certificate," he whispered to her.

She slightly moved in bed, and the streaks of light flashed on the walls. "Your mother called... She said your sister is pregnant with high stocks. The family is happy now. She wanted the cloud back..."

"The cloud doesn't matter, Lithia. It never did! We need my name on the star's birth certificate. You're going to give birth tonight."

"Tonight?" She looked at both of them with surprise. "So soon?"

"Yes, yes, darling! We're going to be parents again! But we do need my name on the certificate. Please think about it!"

"I've been thinking about it... and you must think about it, too. Are you sure you want your name on the star's birth certificate?"

"Why are you asking? You know my answer,

don't you?"

"Oh, of course I do! Still... you should think about it. I failed your family once with the wave, and now the star's coming... I'll never give anything useful, anything you'd proudly show to your family or your friends. You still have a chance to change your mind... I can raise it by myself... If your name is on the certificate it's forever! It's not like with the wave. Do you realize it? This would be forever!"

That night she gave birth to the star. There were only two witnesses present—he and the Astronomer.

"So, what's the name of the father," the Astronomer asked, holding the birth certificate.

"David. The father's name is David," she replied, feeding the star with milk from the Milky Way.

J. J. Steinfeld

The Furtive Men Perform Nightly at the Wretched Street Bar

I still can't get that writer woman out of my mind. It's been almost a year since we were last together, since she disappeared, but I'm not worried about her. I know that wherever in the world she is, that woman knows exactly what she's doing. It took me a long time to understand why she came to the stinking little bar I work at, but I sure found out. She called it the Wretched Street Bar and I liked that name a hell of a lot more than the Lilac Avenue Lounge, which it's been called for longer than anyone I know can remember. She also gave the house band a great name: The Furtive Men. I'd like to see that writer woman again, but that's impossible, as impossible as me ever quitting this place I work at and getting a regular daytime job.

But she's still mine, in memory at least, in the book of hers that I've read twenty times. It was four years ago when I first saw that writer woman. I spotted her right away in the crowded bar that night. The house band was playing—they always attracted a strange crowd, loud, screaming, a weird bunch of the costumed and odd—and there she was at a table of people a little too respectable for the place, the spectator-type I call them. Once or twice to the Wretched Street Bar and they've had enough. Out to see how the lowlife element of society drinks away their nights. She was dressed as straight as could be and looking like she belonged in an office with air-conditioning and large well-tended plants. Right in the middle of the noise and craziness of the bar, she was writing on a sheet of paper, taking notes actually. Later I found out she was writing her cultural review column for one of the newspapers in town, but how she got the Wretched Street Bar and culture mixed up, I'll never know. She told me another time, when we got to know each other, that for the newspaper's Saturday arts-supplement "culture" was very loosely defined. I might have been one of the only ones who either worked or drank at the bar to see her column—good thing too, the way she described the boorish, loutish patrons and the decibel-crazed, mind-rattling band. Yet she kept coming back, without her well-dressed, gawking friends, sitting alone at a small table and writing, always neatly dressed. It took me a while to comment about that column to her, and when I did she told me that it was only a small part of her work, that she was basically a fiction writer who for extra money did movie, theatre, art, and restaurant reviews, in addition to her weekly cultural column, until her larger projects came to fruition. Like a book? I asked. Yes, like a book, she said, and smiled in that way that would stay in my mind for hours.

After I had waited on her a few times, she said to me, "You weren't here last night," starting the first personal conversation we had.

"Wednesday is my day off," I told her.

"And Sunday?" she said.

"Sunday, of course."

"Then I won't come here on Wednesdays

anymore," she told me as if she were making some big religious declaration.

"Wednesdays are like any other day around here," I tried to tell her.

She changed the subject by asking real intensely, "Aren't you curious about me?"

"Sure, but I don't meddle in other people's business."

"That's admirable."

"It's how I get by in this miserable boozing hole...."

I had waited on her several times before, watched her, saw her watching me, but we hadn't exchanged more than a few barroom, talk-above-the-sound-of-the-band pleasantries. The Furtive Men could sure play loud, and they got louder as the night went on, louder and raunchier.

When I brought her another drink, a beer, which I thought was odd, I don't know why, except that she looked like she should be drinking expensive mixed drinks, she glanced to a corner table and asked, "Does that happen often?"

"The odd time, when they get really loaded," I told her, looking at the couple who were necking heavily, and about to make love in the corner discreetly, well, as discreetly as you could in a crowded bar with the Furtive Men playing loud as can be.

I didn't want to mention that there were dirty little rooms in the back where, for a few bucks, an amorous couple could get to know each other better. That stuff didn't bother me at all. My job was steady, the tips okay, and I coped with life just fine doing my five nights a week at the Wretched Street Bar. The writer woman found out the score soon enough and seemed to consider it no more interesting than if she had discovered there was a backroom sewing circle.

In the beginning she asked me lots of questions, watched me all the time, along with everything else in the noisy, poorly-lit bar, and I thought that maybe she was writing a whole series of cultural columns for newspapers all over the planet. I couldn't understand then who the hell would care about the bar, unless it was people who got off on reading about misery. To me the Wretched Street Bar was the end of the world, but I was used to it. And with my screwed-up background, working where I did kept me from blowing all apart again.

She was friendly, to me at least, and we hit it off pretty well. I stopped trying to figure out why she liked talking to me and just started to consider her a good friend, even if our friendship existed only in the Wretched Street Bar. Yet no matter how long I knew her, she was always saying something to surprise me.

"You're a dear, beautiful boy;" she told me somewhere about the second week.

"I'm no boy," I argued, feeling that I've been around, never really appreciating that I looked so young.

"No, you're not," she said, looking at me, all over me, but not in a bad way. I told her I'd be twenty-six in a couple of months and she asked me more questions. She was amazed when I told her this was the only steady job I've ever had, that I'd been at the bar almost three full years, but who's counting. It didn't amaze her nearly as much when I told her I'd spent time in jail and used to be into drugs. I'd swear those revelations made her like me more, but I couldn't be sure. I don't touch any drugs these days, even booze is off-limits to me, and she told me that self-destructiveness didn't suit me. I told her it used to be my middle name, that I didn't used to care if I lived or died, but now I'm not disappointed when I open my eyes in the morning.

It didn't take long, maybe a month, before she started to bring me little presents. The first one, I remember clear as day, really caught me by surprise. She handed me this fancily wrapped package, took it right out of her nice leather briefcase, and I was baffled. Even after all I've seen in the bar, a fancily wrapped package from a beautifully dressed, sophisticated woman customer still managed to throw me for a loop.

I put the package on my serving tray, in the center of all the empty glasses I had gathered up, and she told me to open it up later. In the kitchen area, my back to a couple of bored waiters smoking a joint, I opened my gift, and came back with a big grin on my face, neglecting some of the orders I was supposed to deliver.

"You said you like to stay up late and read," she said when I got back to her table.

"You didn't have to do this," I told her, examining my new little reading lamp, the kind you can attach to a book and use in bed.

"I wanted to."

"Your tips are real generous."

"You noticed."

"I keep track."

"You write down the amounts?"

"Naw, in my brain. I got a good head for numbers," I said with a bit of pride. Then I told her, "You're the best tipper—consistently, I mean—I've ever had."

"You're most courteous and helpful."

"I'm only doing my job."

As I walked away to an upset customer's shout of "Hey stupid, bring me my drink," I told the writer woman I would use my little reading lamp that night. And every night. I still do.

I figure she brought me about one present a week: clothing, magazines, books, knickknacks. My apartment is like a gift shop with all the stuff she gave me. I got to expect the gifts, even though I'd never know what night of the week they would come. Sometimes it would be more than a little something, like the time she got me ten pairs of suspenders, all of different styles and colours. That was one of my favourite gifts. I always wore suspenders at work, my trademark, sort of.

Then one night, when I was really getting used to her, the writer woman threw me again. "I'm forty-seven-years old today," she told me after her first beer of the night, then quickly ordered another.

"I'd never have guessed. I mean, I'd say you were in your late thirties, early forties at the most."

"Forty-seven is important to me," she said in a real solemn way.

"Well, it's time for a celebration. Your drinks are all on me
tonight," I said, giving her my best don't-let-life-get-to-you voice.

"I might drink you into the poorhouse."

"You're a pretty tame drinker," I contradicted her with a smile.

"I'll have to change my image tonight."

"You never get drunk, not in this bar."

"So this will be my debut in a major inebriation production."

"Forty-seven isn't the end of the world," I told her. "You are one great-looking woman."

"Both my mother and my father died when they were forty-seven, two years apart though," she explained, not a hell of a lot of expression on her face when she talked about her folks.

I offered my sympathy, but she told me in an unemotional way, "That was a long time ago, don't concern yourself. The symbolic significance of that age doesn't escape me."

"I never really had a chance to know my parents," I said, but she already knew that. My father had beaten my mother to death when I was six, and I never saw the bastard after he got locked away. The writer woman had questioned me on other nights, asked me all about my life, jotted down her notes. Peculiar thing, she hardly ever talked to anyone else in the bar, but those beautiful dark eyes of hers took everything in.

"If you get drunk, watch out for the horny guys around here," I warned her, only a little jokingly.

"You always take care of me."

"What's a good waiter for, if he can't look after his best customer."

She got good and drunk that night, but I got her into a cab and was thankful she hadn't hurt herself worse. When I went back to clean up her table, there was a twenty-buck tip. Usually it was five or ten, but that night it was twenty, and she hadn't had to pay for any of her birthday drinks. After that night, it was always a twenty-buck tip from the writer woman, no matter how much or how little she drank. Some nights her tip was bigger than her bill for drinks. I told her she didn't have to be so extravagant with her money, but she continued to leave the big tips, not to mention the once-a-week presents. According to my calculations, during the three years the writer woman came to the bar she left me nearly fifteen thousand in tips, not counting how much the presents were worth. Where she got the money I didn't know but she sure wasn't ever short of cash.

Next time in she brought me a handful of magazines I liked, mostly stuff about cars and sports. I started skimming through them and said, "I never finished high school, but I've become a real keen reader." I was always defensive about my lack of education. To be accurate, I let the writer woman know that I'd been kicked out of school.

"You sound most intelligent to me," she said.

"I read more than a lot of people and I spend time in the library just about every afternoon, before coming to work."

"Ah, an autodidact," she blurted out, like she'd finally identified some mysterious animal.

"I don't know that one."

"It means self-taught."

"That's a good name for me—autodidact. Better than your kind hearted neighbourhood booze dispenser."

I became more and more curious about the writer woman, but she always avoided telling me too much about herself, only asking me questions, sometimes real personal, but I didn't mind answering them most of the time. About the third or fourth week after meeting her I had started cutting out her Saturday cultural review columns, and any other writings of hers in magazines and newspapers I could find, and putting them in a scrapbook. For some time I didn't want to tell her what I was doing.

I noticed she started to drink more, but I always made sure no one would bother her in the bar and I'd get her safely into a cab at the end of the night. She usually stayed until closing time or near to it. On one occasion, when she was heavy-duty drunk and I was trying to help her up, she said, "I've had a good, privileged life—but not a life I've been terribly satisfied with. You understand what I'm trying to get across?"

"Maybe you want too much out of life," I told the writer woman, deciding that I should sit down with her for a little while.

"That's not it at all. I'd like not to want anything. To let my mind relax occasionally."

"Then close your eyes and do it."

"Inside me," she said, pointing to her head, "it's like a furious storm that simply won't calm down. I look in the mirror and can't see any of that turmoil, that obsessiveness, but it's there inside me. Whether I like it or not, I can't be any other way."

"People ask me when I'm going to leave this cruddy excuse for a bar, find a day job in some bright, sunny place with a thousand windows, and I say I like it here—even though I complain my damn head off. Follow me?"

"We're not that different," she said, and asked me to get her another beer. I told her she'd had enough, and she got mad at me for the first time. Pushing away my friendly concern, the writer woman threatened to go to an after-hours club to finish off more drinks, to fall into the clutches of who knows who, and I gave her another beer, grumbling about her stubbornness. After she got even more drunk, she kept saying, "Life imitating art, art imitating life," until she passed out. I sat with her until she came to, and helped her get a cab, as usual. I felt something real strong about that writer woman, but I couldn't describe it or really begin to let her know how much I cared for her. It didn't matter how many times I'd seen her, I always looked forward to the writer woman coming into the bar, and hated my days off when I wouldn't see her. Sometimes I looked for her on the streets downtown, but I never saw her during the day, as if it were against one of Nature's laws that we meet outside the Wretched Street Bar.

But I could count on the writer woman being in at night, even if it was late because she had gone to see a play or movie. We reached an anniversary at the Wretched Street Bar, and I brought her a present. I didn't know what to get her at first, but I spent a long time thinking about it until the right gift hit me.

"What's this?" she said, after I put the box down in front of her on the table.

"A present, isn't that obvious?"

"I'm the present-giver," she told me, almost like she was scolding me, then said in a friendly tone, "The information you give me is more than enough."

"But it's our anniversary."

"Our anniversary?" she said, not hiding that she was puzzled. "One year to the day since you first came into the bar."

"One year, yes. I should have known." She seemed

to concentrate on that thought for quite a while.

I wanted her to open the box right away, but she scribbled some notes down instead. She wrote in a strange kind of shorthand and I could never make out what she was writing. Some nights she wrote pages and pages of notes. "One entire year," she repeated.

When I returned with her drink, she had the box open, and was smiling like she'd just won the biggest lottery jackpot.

"You gave me a whole bunch of suspenders once, remember?" I told her as she inspected her gift with a little girl's delight in her eyes.

She tried each one of the fifteen pens and smiled even wider, the delight getting stronger if that was possible. Those were nice pens and a couple were pretty expensive. I had gone around to a lot of stores to make sure the pens were all different. One of the pens, the fanciest one, had set me back over seventy-five bucks. I couldn't remember ever doing anything that nuts before, unless it was in the old days when I was high on dope.

"I gave you only ten pairs of suspenders," she said, touching each pen individually.

"I wanted to outdo you, just once."

She laughed, and got back to writing notes, using one of her new pens. After that night, the writer woman always brought one or two of the pens with her. She told me she wouldn't write with an ordinary pen ever again. My pens, she claimed with a straight face, were magical and inspirational.

The writer woman was in particularly good spirits on her forty-eighth birthday, telling me that now she had no fears about not living a long life.

"Since I was in my twenties, when my parents died, I thought I'd live only as long as they had: forty-seven. Even as rational as I am, that grim thought ate into my mind and reason with an unholy persistence. Now I know I'm protected."

Our life together, if you could call it that, went on through a second anniversary and a third—and a pretty joyful fiftieth birthday celebration for the writer woman—and I thought we would go on forever like a compatible married couple, until a few months after our third anniversary together, a week after she had turned fifty, she said something that completely floored me: "I want you to come home with me after work tonight." Her look was serious and came awfully close to scaring me.

I stood there stunned, nearly spilled the drinks off my tray.

"I have something to give you. An important gift," she said, trying to snap me out of my bewilderment.

In the bar, sitting down next to her, I didn't know what she had in mind, about going home with her I mean. I used to think of her sexually, but that had faded, as if wanting her in that way might ruin the incredible relationship we had. I had come to count on her presence, her words, her shorthand scribbling of notes, her gifts, her tips, the scrapbook I kept of her columns and reviews, getting her into a cab when she was ready to leave, seeing her come into the bar sometime between nine and eleven nearly every night.

"You must come home with me tonight," she insisted, and I can vaguely remember nodding my head yes. So many thoughts went through my head then that I could barely sort them out. I felt like I had been walking real careful along a narrow ledge, and all of a sudden had started running like mad.

"It's immeasurable what I owe you," she said, and it didn't sound like bullshit coming from the writer woman.

"You've given me way too much already," I told her.

She sat and waited until I had finished cleaning up. We wound up being the last two in the bar, except for the band, who never seemed to leave.

In the back of the cab she sat close to me, but only patted my hands and touched my cheeks, as if I were a child needing to be reassured that he would not be left alone in the dark. I wanted to touch her, to hold her, but something held me back, even frightened me.

The cab went a real far distance and the fare was steep. I was both confused and excited as hell, and I couldn't say how long the ride was or even guess how to find the place.

We stopped in front of a small house way outside the city, a house surrounded by a few acres of land.

Inside, nothing seemed unusual. It was neat, clean, lots of books and bookshelves. She put on an old record—a million years from the Furtive Men... Beethoven or Bach, I think—and left me sitting on the couch in the living room. I couldn't believe how jumbled my thinking was while she was gone.

When she came back into the room she held a hardback book in her hands and gave it a little kiss before handing it to me. I was almost afraid to take the book. Then I nearly dropped it when I read the title: The Furtive Men Perform Nightly at the Wretched Street Bar.

"So, that's why you came to the dive," I said, not really pleased with my new insight.

"Look at the dedication," she told me.

I fumbled through the first few pages and found it. The dedication was to me, with the inscription, "The man who gave me what I wanted most." Those simple words seemed to counteract real quick any feelings I had of having been used, studied like an insect in a jar. If I had been an insect, then I was one who had not fought to get away from its life in the jar.

The writer woman and I made love that night and, I don't know how else to describe it, my body and heart whirled with happiness I didn't think possible. Afterwards, I kept opening the book, reading sentences here and there, not really able to concentrate on the words. I couldn't get over that she would set a whole novel, over 400 pages, in that worthless hole of a bar where I worked.

Then she really gave it to me: "The novel is about you. It's your story."

"I'm nothing, I'm a goddamn nothing," I told her, no false modesty in what I had said, but she pointed to the book. I brushed the cover with my fingertips, as if I was trying to communicate with something alive. We made love again, but before it was even sunrise the writer woman told me I had to leave. I was trying to argue that I should be allowed to stay for the day, after three years of seeing each other that was only fair, but she had already called a cab for me. Losing hold of the real world, I even thought about living with her, of us being lovers who woke up every morning in each other's arms.

The next day I waited for her to come into the bar,

paying attention to very little else. She didn't show up. Night after night, and the writer woman wasn't there. Her columns and reviews stopped appearing in the newspapers and magazines, and none of the people she had written for had a clue where she had gone. I also called the publisher of her book, long distance, but they dealt through her agent, who wasn't likely to be any more helpful since, they said, he had always been evasive concerning any details about her life. The writer woman's publisher and her editor didn't even know her real name, only the pen name that she had used for the novel.

I started going to other bars in the city, looking for her, arriving at work late or leaving early. I reread the novel, went through the scrapbook daily. Eventually I broke through my stupidity and started to put things together.

I sense that she is writing her next novel somewhere, probably in another bar in some other city, maybe even in a different country, far away from everything I know. It didn't take me long to get back into my routine at the Wretched Street Bar, dealing with what I knew best. What's hardest for me to understand, what confuses me all to hell, is that I love her more now than ever. And the biggest kicker in my whole remembering and thinking about that writer woman is that I keep waiting for her to return.

Dustin Grayson

Best Head Ever

The entrance of St. Pius X High School felt Paul's presence long before he strolled into the building. The windows rattled, banisters shook, and heads turned to the cacophony of sound pouring in through the cracks in the doorway. When the noise reached a deafening pitch, and the pinned up ninth grade artwork started to fall off the wall, Paul swung the door open and greeted himself to the band of teachers, administrators, and students that were gathering around. He only had one hand to wave, high five, and shake with because the other was securing an enormous Magnavox D8443 Ghetto Blaster boombox. The taunt, alliterative, straight gangsta verses of Public Enemy discharged from the rattling speakers. The musical selection was incidental. If he had found Boyz II Men, Journey, or Heart, his entrance would have taken a different note. On this warm autumn day, a heavy set white boy with uncontrollable curly hair walked into his school and secured his notoriety forever.

  Brian Hughes did not like to make an entrance. Attention made him sweat. His pink skin would blanch and turn the sour color of buttermilk. He was a teenager, looked exactly like one, and was nothing short of ordinary. He walked into St. Pius the same time as Paul, and while he had both hands open, no one shook, clapped, or embraced them. The only classmates who knew him were Paul and Katie Lee Marcovich, the girl he has loved ever since preschool.

Mr. Northbrook was the school's vice principal. During his tour in the Gulf War, he had developed an exaggerated sense of discipline and an affinity for polishing his shoes. He was in his office staining his pair of Steve Madden's when the bass line of "Bring the Noise" caused him to accidentally swipe the laces with the dark oil. He swore to himself, pulled on his moist shoes, and charged out of the office. After cutting through the crowd, he seized the offending stereo and gutted the batteries. Jabbing a thick finger into Paul's chest, Northbrook said that this sort of behavior will not be tolerated. After all, St. Pius X was not a public school.

He tossed the stereo's carcass into the trash, and returned to his office with a swift, proud gait. Little crescent moons of black polish trailed behind him, marking the floor.

When the door to the Administration Department closed, the students broke into laughter.

Mrs. Allenbee was the only teacher at St. Pius X not affiliated with the church. It was her Maplewood Community Theater performance in *Jesus Christ Superstar* that motivated Father Brown, the head of the school, to both forgive her trespasses and offer her a job.

Her classroom was unoccupied for a majority of the school year. This vacancy, however, did not cause any alarm or concern, as it was well known her students preferred to practice on the stage in the school's auditorium. The theater had more space, better lighting, and an opportunity to imagine a room of two hundred people celebrating your every move.

Paul loved this room. He would come in on Thursday evenings with Brian and Katie. They would adjust the lights, cue up sound effects, and stock the smoke machine with heaps of dry ice. Thursday nights were sacred. Their performances on the following day were a consummation of the love they held for each other. They were a unit, always choosing each other as their scene partners. When an assignment would only allow two to a scene, Paul would graciously opt out and let Brian share the scene with Katie.

Brian's tragedy was that he was not Katie's boyfriend. Denny McCarthy was. Denny was tall. He was fit. His skin was always clear, and his letterman jacket had so many varsity letters on it you couldn't see the wool underneath. Brian had no hope.

Last week, he and Katie Lee ran through the love declaration scene in *Cyrano de Bergerac*. Brian related a lot to Cyrano. He had told Katie he loved her so many times, but he could never unearth the courage to tell her as himself, in his own voice, using his own words. If the words had ever freed themselves from his tight-lipped grasp, they could only be sounded if they were spoken from underneath a false nose, an accent, or a whisper she had no hope to hear.

Today, he told her she completed him.

After the day's last performance, Mrs. Allenbee took the stage to give the next week's assignment. She swallowed whatever liquid lingered in her throat and announced the next week's assignment.

Brian opened his planner to take notes on the project. Everyone listened intently.

"My husband has reminded me that next week is

Valentine's Day, or *Saint* Valentine's Day, as it were here," she said. "In the spirit of this sacred and wonderful holiday, which guides us annually to demonstrate our love for the people we hold closest in our lives, I hereby direct the class to couple up..."

While she spoke, Brian jotted down in his planner, "holiday - duet."

"...and perform a kissing scene."

Brian's pencil snapped.

"This scene should not be pornographic, but endearing and charming. The films of Richard Curtis should be a good start."

With one of the ends of the broken pencil, Brian wrote, "Cute + English accent = A."

"But that's just a start. You could choose from any movie or play you please, as long as it is not anything from *Fatal Attraction* – or rather anything from Michael Douglas. You *must* kiss. And unless you can prove you've got some form of Hepatitis, you are not getting out of it." With that last note, and on cue, the lights dimmed, letting Mrs. Allenbee take sanctuary in her locked office, which was fortunately nowhere near the auditorium.

Brian was terrified.

Her assignment affected the rest of the class in much the same way. A solid thump had rippled through the room and the students were quickly counted and divided amongst their sex. The class learned what Paul already knew: there were twelve guys to eleven girls. He was the odd man out. In the past, he was granted the option of acting out both parts or performing with Mrs. Allenbee. He gulped.

The only pupil left unfazed was Katie Lee. Like Brian, she too liked to take down the assignments. Currently, she was penciling his name into her planner. She turned to him, hoping to make eye contact, which often proved difficult, and asked, "How's Saturday at three? I'm free after the Shermer meet. Brian?"

He was looking at her through his fingers, which at the moment were stuck to his face. He couldn't figure out how to pry them loose. The puzzle was too challenging. "Hmm?" he asked, pretending he hadn't heard.

"Hey," she whispered as she gently took hold on his hands. They warmed to her touch and let go, freeing his face before settling into his lap. Her hands stayed. "You wanna come over Saturday?" She was silhouetted by one of the warm auditorium lights and her blonde hair glowed bright, almost pink. She could feel his pulse quicken.

He nodded.

"Good," she said, before letting go and leaving. As if a tourniquet was released, a wealth of feeling flooded Brian's body. He let the endorphins rush onto him like lazy waves on a beach, tickling his feet, legs, and fingers.

The afternoon announcements played on through the intercom and the class had all but departed. Sitting one behind the other, Brian and Paul stared ahead in traps of thought. Brian wished he could burn that last image of Katie into his cornea, so he could see her always and before everything.

Paul was fixing his position on how sock puppetry was due a triumphant and spectacular return to the stage.

Brian had killed 37 aliens before Paul was able to pry a word from him. Brian's lips were locked shut. Her invitation shook the columns of his composition, and a lifetime of repressed and evaded desires had taken hold of him.

He was going to kiss her. And all he could think to himself was, "Shit."

The boys spent a majority of their Friday nights at Lazy Asteroids, a rare teen-friendly establishment that featured a *Ms. Pac-man* tournament on Fridays. They enjoyed coming to the arcade at this time as most of the games were left vacant.

Once they had taken Katie to the arcade to celebrate their presentation of *Evil Dead II* (Paul's turn as the possessed hand garnered a three-minute standing ovation). She secured first place on the *Area 51* scorecard in her first attempt, and was never invited back. Brian and Paul spent each subsequent Friday trying to best her score, and have not yet, after many months and attempts, posted better numbers.

"I think the trick is in blowing up the barrels," Paul offered, hoping Brian would open up. He hated when Brian clammed up. He had cracked out once before. A freshman named Sara Griffins asked him out to the Sadie Hawkins dance. His consciousness did not resurface until two days later when Paul, inspired by *Jacob's Ladder*, forced him into a bath of ice water.

Brian didn't respond to the advice. He was focused, and was playing even better than he usually could. Every flammable object was ignited, every goon decimated, and every weapon upgrade was seized.

The level ended, and the next mission was loading.

"I was thinking we should get Paisan's afterwards. How's that sound?" Paul asked.

No response.

"It's okay, we don't have to go. How's about Chan's? You like eggrolls there."

Brian continued to ignore him. The new level began, and Brian kept his killing streak.

Paul's anger was building, and he was tired of having to treat Brian like some African violet, where even the slightest touch would wilt and deform him. When Brian's score neared the record, and his eyes were burning from unwiped sweat, Paul stepped in front of the screen.

"What're you doing?" Brian shrieked and tried to aim around him, but his friend's head was too large. Paul instinctively raised his hands. From behind his left thumb, a piranha-faced beast sneaked out and slashed at Brian.

The screen prompted: GAME OVER.

Brian dropped his arms to sides. They were heavy and sore, near lifeless. His focus shifted from the screen, which was announcing his second place standing, to Paul's bashful, lipless smile. "Sorry, dude."

Brian's eyes narrowed, and he stomped at Paul's feet.

"Hey!" Paul cried, seemingly both annoyed and humored. He stamped back, and the boys continued to bruise the other's feet until they both fell down in pain and laughter.

Resting on the floor, they leaned their backs on the gaming machine.

"Three more points," Brian pondered out loud.

"You really want to beat Katie's score? It'd kind of defeat the purpose of coming here."

A boastful shout and a pitiful cry came from within the heart of the Ms. Pac-man crowd. Seconds later, a shrunken man teetered out from within the mob, which was busy cheering their new champion.

Brian gestured to the man. "No, that's why we're here."

They exchanged glances and laughed.

"It's amazing," Paul said, "how someone can make something trivial their whole world."

"Like those guys you see who come here every Friday to beat some girl's score."

"Just like that."

"Just like that," Brian echoed.

"Brian, I need you to talk to me. 'Help *me* help *you*.'" Paul laid a hand on Brian's shoulder, trying to comfort him, but Brian turned away.

"I don't need consoling, Paul." His voice was quivering.

"I know."

"I have loved this girl for literally all of my life. Seriously, all of it. And the only time I have ever been able to admit it is when I am pretending to be someone else. Someone who is distinctly not me." Brian looked down at his hands, and began to toy with the bottom of his T-shirt. "It feels like I'm lying to her every time I say I love her, you know, even though I do."

"How are you lying to her?"

"Because they're not my words. They're someone else's. If I am going to kiss her, I wanna kiss her as me, and not as some character, not for some scene. Not for some teacher or a grade." He glanced up at Paul to see if he was smiling at him, mocking him in some way, but he wasn't. "I wanna kiss her for me. As me, you know? Naked before her."

"Naked?"

"Not literally. Look, I know I'm making too much of this, but I don't care." He took a breath and felt his stomach. "Let's get up, all right? Paisan's sounds pretty good right now."

The boys got up and went and had some pizza. Sitting at their table, they talked excitedly about *World of Warcraft*. They talked about *Iron Man 2*. They talked about going back to the arcade next Friday to beat that near-impossible score. For the rest of the evening, not once did they talk about Mrs. Allenbee's class, Katie Lee Marcovich, or how Brian was going to kiss her.

Katie's house was the latest Frank Lloyd Wright imitation. The house was so beautiful, and so well incorporated into its environment, it took Brian twenty minutes to find the front door. This was after the struggle he had just to find the property. The home, and the road leading up to it, was so new Brian was unable to find directions on either MapQuest or Google Maps. He eventually found the house only because a fallen tree blocked the road he wanted to take, forcing him and his father's BMW down an uneven and unstable gravel route, which invariably led him straight to her home.

She greeted him outside the house with a hug and a kiss on the cheek. She was wearing an over-sized St. Pius XXL long-sleeve with acid-wash jeans. Her hair was still wet from a shower Brian tried hard to not imagine. She led him up a sprawl of free-standing stairs to her bedroom.

Her room was not as he expected, but more as he

remembered. While he had never been in this room before, the objects within were deeply familiar. A number of them were gifts he had given her, including a series of Troll dolls that lined her vanity mirror. He picked up one of the Trolls, a pink one with short hair and blue eyeliner, and pondered it.

"I always wanted to be a cosmetologist," Katie said. "You knew that, right? I wanted to do makeup for the stars. Only I never had the courage to work on real people. These dolls were good sports. Never complained once."

Brian sat the doll down in its place. "I had no idea you kept them."

"You kidding? They're my favorite. I'd like to think I kept everything, but, you know, moves are hard. Dad likes to keep the property value high. So, it's hard to know where we'll be in a year."

"You remember the one in Highland Peace? You had Rainbow Bright window blinds and a Ninja Turtles shower curtain."

"We used to take baths together in that tub. You remember?"

"No," he said, even though he did.

"Well, I remember. I've seen you naked, Brian. I hope puberty has treated you well."

Brian didn't know what to do with that, especially after she winked. He gulped and pretended not to understand, which was true enough.

"Enough with the nostalgia, we have work to do."

"Yes ma'am."

Katie was anxious to show him the scene she had picked out. She knew he would love it. Taking him by the hand, she led him around her desk to in front of her computer screen. "Watch this," she said before playing a video entitled, "Best Kiss Ever."

What played before him were two scenes from an old movie. In the first scene, Ingrid Bergman and Cary Grant were exchanging innuendos. She said, "I have a chicken in the icebox, and you're eating it." He asked, "What about all the washing up afterward?" "We'll eat with our fingers." Each line in the scene was broken up by quick, longing kisses. "When I don't love you," he said, "I'll let you know." "You haven't said anything." "Actions speak louder than words." The scene was great, full of kisses and all of the words Brian wanted to say.

The second scene Katie played was much darker. In the clip, Bergman told Grant how much she loved him, but he was keeping quiet. He had dark secrets to keep.

Brian's eyes drifted from the screen to a framed photograph of Katie and Denny. They were in a park, knee-deep in a pile of amber leaves. The photo must have been taken around a year ago. He was lifting her up in his arms, and they were smiling to the camera. Brian tried to find a glimmer of boredom or unhappiness in her face, but found none. She looked happy.

"It's called *Notorious*," Katie said. "I Googled, 'Best Kiss Scene,' and this is what came up again and again. In the scene, I'm Alicia and you're Devlin. Movie's by Hitchcock. Remember when we did that scene from *Psycho*?"

"I still can't believe Allenbee let us run a hose along the stage."

They smiled as they remembered the mess they

made and trouble they caused.

"I thought we'd do something from *Love Actually*. I do a pretty good H-h-hugh Grant."

She wrinkled her nose and shook her head. "Too predictable. She gave the whole Richard Curtis thing away in class. Everyone's gonna do it. Unless we're that naked couple doing the movie we've got no shot at surprising her."

Despite his shyness, Brian had no problem being naked, as long as she'd be naked too.

"And I'm not getting naked," she said.

"Oh."

They tried to arrange the act inside of her bedroom, but the room was too small. A change of setting was a relief to Brian as the room's glass walls – and Katie's proximity – were making him nauseous.

Excited and inspired, Katie said, "I know where we should go. Follow me!" She rushed out the door, and through the wall Brian could see her turn down the hall and make her way down the spiral of stairs.

He ran after her, following her down the stairs into her living room, where original works by Richard Prince and Bridget Riley hung. Underneath the Plexiglas floor, a thin stream of water followed over flat green rocks.

"Hurry up!" she called before heading into the large kitchen. Over the stovetop, Katie's mother, Natasha, was working a bowl of eggs with a steel whisk. Surprised at the kids' sudden appearance, Natasha quickly wiped her face, leaving smudges of flour on her cheek. "Hi, Brian," she said, giving him a smile. Her smile was familiar, and Brian realized how much Katie looked like her mother.

"Mrs. Marcovich," Brian answered.

Katie took a towel and cleaned the flour off her mother's face. "Mom, would you mind if Brian and I rehearsed on the deck?"

Natasha's head rattled and shoulders shrugged. "No. Sure. You kids have fun."

After wiping another smudge off her mother's face, she replied, "You too."

Katie motioned to Brain and led him to a large patio.

The deck was projected out over a ten-foot cliff. The stream from under the living room exited as a small waterfall under their feet.

"Isn't it fantastic out here? I just love it. I come out here all the time to do my homework, but I can never concentrate. It's just too beautiful. You know what I mean?" The fresh, cool wind teased her hair, and her skin tightened and braced.

"I do," Brian replied, truthfully.

"I was thinking the choreography was more like a dance than anything," Katie said. "Calling off numbers may be the best way of doing this."

Brian agreed. He would have agreed to anything at this point.

They started from the top. As they moved through the space, Katie would do counts of four. When it came time for a kiss, she would assign the kiss a number and not actually give Brian one.

The scene was easy to learn. Katie had most of the dialogue, and a lot of the things he wanted himself to say to Katie mirrored those Devlin said to Alicia. He understood Devlin's inability to express himself, and the pain and consequences that stemmed from this impotency.

After rehearsing for the better part of an hour, they decided to take a break. Katie went into the kitchen and returned with two cold bottles of Lipton tea. The drink was refreshing, and Brian was hoping the lemon would cover the smell of the leftover pizza he had for lunch.

The landscape really was beautiful. He hoped he would be invited back. Standing close to Katie, and drinking his tea, Brian felt a moment of relief and calm. He gripped the ledge and inhaled. The air was fresh and noted with the rich, dusty fragrance of aging brush. The forest trees were filled with brilliant red leaves. Brian knew their vibrancy would only last a day. If he would look again tomorrow, he knew he would see much less beauty. The leaves' pigment would have faded down to a dull umber, and many of the leaves would have fallen from their branches, only to rest on ungrateful earth.

"I wanna be where you are," Katie said.

"I'm here."

She pressed her lips and nodded pleasingly at his answer. She turned back to the view, to see what he could see; and, of course, she could.

"This sure is a lot better than my view," Brian said. "I get to look out at Ms. Grasinsky mowing her lawn in her bathrobe."

"Bathrobe?"

"Yeah. It's white, except for all the grass stains along the bottom."

Brian's nervousness returned to him. He still hadn't found the right words. Adrenaline crept inside of him. His knees and hands shook. His stomach clenched, and he started to sweat.

Quoting the scene, Katie asked, "'Come on, Mr. D. What's darkening your brow?'" Using the end of her shirt sleeve, she dabbed his forehead.

"Nothing. I just got cold all-of-a-sudden."

Brushing hair away from his eyes, she corrected him. "You're supposed to answer, 'After dinner.'"

Brian tried to say the line indifferently, but he could not. He pleaded, "After dinner."

"Are you sure?" Katie asked, breaking away from the script.

He shook his head.

Without any conscious desire or awareness, their bodies had moved together. They have always had natural magnetism, but have rarely dared to stand this close to one another.

"When you do, let me know. Until then, 'You haven't said anything.'"

The breeze was becoming colder; the only warmth could be felt between them. Their eyes were glistening, and their skin flushed. She was so close to him now, he could smell her breath, her hair, and she too smelled of autumn.

He said his line.

"And three," she counted. "This is where we kiss."

A loud, sharp *clang* came from inside the kitchen, which sounded exactly like the noise a cookie sheet might make if dropped on a Plexiglas floor.

On the following Monday morning, Brian and Paul went to school. Paul had tried on the drive to pry details of Brian's afternoon with Katie, but was largely unsuccessful. Brian wouldn't have minded opening up, but he himself was unsure as to what had happened. He was certain they leaned in close together, spoke of kissing, and that he almost lost his nerve, but didn't. After that moment, all Brian remembered was the smell of Katie's shampoo and the taste of dark chocolate. They did not kiss, but during rehearsals today – he'd get another chance.

They took their seats in Allenbee's classroom. Katie hadn't yet arrived, and as the minute bell tolled, Brian's anxiousness returned with a familiar weight. He exchanged glances with Paul. "Call her," he whispered.

Paul shrugged and texted, "Whr R U?" There was no reply and the class began.

In the middle of Mrs. Allenbee's lecture on *Hamlet* and post-modernism, Katie entered the room. Brian sighed, relieved. He tried to establish eye-contact with her, but she looked confused, embarrassed, and frustrated. She sat down in the closest free seat, which was across the room from where she usually sat, where Brian and Paul were sitting. Mrs. Allenbee tried to continue her lecture, but she was interrupted immediately by Denny entering the room.

She tilted her head at Denny, and asked, "How did I earn the pleasure of your company?"

He took out a wadded up note from his jeans. After unraveling the paper, and smoothing it out on his knee, he presented it to Mrs. Allenbee. She read the note and motioned for Denny to take a seat. He did so next to Katie Lee. He rested an arm over the back of her chair.

Throughout the rest of the lecture, Brian tried to get Katie's attention. He whispered and waved his hands, but had no luck. He was in the middle of making a spit ball with a broken pen and some paper, when Allenbee moved on from her lecture to the kissing assignment. She went around the room and asked the students who their partners were and what scene they will be performing. Most of the students announced they will be doing a scene from *Love Actually*. When it came time for Katie to answer for which scene she would be performing, Denny answered for her. He said, "*Notorious*."

At first, Brian thought it was a joke. Some elaborate prank Paul set up. But when he looked over to Paul, Brian saw him frowning. Brian would have fallen out of his chair if Paul hadn't secured him by his collar. He couldn't breathe. When he did, the air tasted sour. The bitterness came from a tear, which, before languishing on his tongue, wet his lips and flushed their color. He tried to smile, but his mouth grimaced like an aged scarecrow.

Brian felt the room shrink. The walls rolled in. Framed posters and mounted props curled and coiled down menacingly over Brian's diminutive body. If he didn't escape right then, his body might've collapsed under the pressure. He'd be crushed. He needed to get away, flee, but then everyone would look at him and know he was crying. Katie would know, and then she would know his secret. But he couldn't stay.

He stood up quickly, too quickly, and the blood rushed from his head. For a moment, the class appeared to be in a haze of blue. With his head down, he whispered his apologies to Allenbee and made his way to the exit. After the door closed behind him, he glimpsed back at Katie through its small square window. She looked at him, at last, and then looked away.

To his horror, he found her sadness.

The south hallway boy's bathroom was not a large room. There was only one sink, two stalls, and not one urinal. Originally, the room had managed three stalls, each of equal size. After the ADA was passed, two of the stalls were combined into a spacious, wheelchair accessible unit. All extra space originally given to the third stall was rescinded. As there were few handicapped students at St. Pius, the stall was mainly occupied by those with sports-related injuries, and others who required the extra leg room for throwing up.

Brian sat down in the lesser unit. Even though he didn't have to relieve himself, he undid his pants and perched himself on the plastic seat. The walls were soft from the countless layers of latex paint, which covered countless years' worth of school boy graffiti.

As there was barely enough room to accommodate his feet, Brian had to saddle his backpack on top of his naked, near-hairless thighs. The weight of the bag gave him comfort. He felt as if the room was flooding. The waters raised high, soaking his shoes, socks and pants. The toilet paper appeared to swell and dissolve into big clumps. Brian clutched his bag, and dug his short nails into the fabric. As the water rushed over his head, he held on firmly. He waited for the flooding to abate. And before too long, it did.

He decided he would be all right. He knew that between him and Paul, an answer would be found– even if they had to kiss each other. As far as he was concerned, Katie was a good friend. He hoped her scene would go well. After all, she gave him a sunset. After all, he still loved her. His shoulders relaxed, his heart steadied, and his eyes dried.

His focus drifted forward and rested on something written on the door. His burning eyes were slow to focus, and he couldn't make out what it was. As if he was looking through an optometrist lens, his vision cleared by degrees until the image set into distinct letters. The bold, black-inked message read: Katie Marcovich - Best Head Ever!

His bag fell from his lap.

Brian had never pretended to understand sex. His knowledge of the female body consisted of cable and illustrations found in his biology textbook. While he didn't understand sexual relationships, and all of their intricacies, he knew what the message meant. It made him shake. Adrenaline snarled through his body, and he did not know what to do. He seized his bag.

At 8:30 am, Mr. Northbrook liked to take a break. Under the guise of offering the hall monitors an extra hand, he'd slip into the south hallway bathroom to read the newspaper while he digested his coffee and fibrous breakfast. He would unwind in the large, private stall, and compose letters for the editor to print in the community reaction section. He loved being published. In the stall, he would bend over the open paper and smell the rich, drying ink of his carefully crafted words. The satisfaction intoxicated him. His morning hallway patrol was the most cherished and valued part of his day spent at St. Pius X.

The waters crept back into the room. As the white foam

sloshed Brian's ankles, the skin along his legs knotted into gooseflesh. His cold and quaking legs were discordant to the heat and steady anger he felt pumping from his heart. He wanted to hit something. As much as he hated its author's intent, their words held a hypnotic and suggestive power that worked to subvert his lionized perception of her. He wanted to throw up, but he was in the wrong stall.

The note blinded him, and he could no longer look ahead. He buried his gaze down at his backpack, and he wondered how long ago the note was written. How many others have read it? How many opinions of Katie been irrevocably changed? The only answer Brian found was that the note must be covered up, wiped off, erased somehow before it could be seen by anyone else.

He tore at the zipper, and reached into the dark pits of his school bag. In the mysterious space under his textbooks, he ran his hand through the coins, clips, pens, and erasers until he found what he was searching for. He came up with a black Sharpie.

Despite how hard he scribbled at the note, no ink would emit from the marker's tip. The graffiti went unhindered. As Brian glared at the words, the ribbons of letters seemed to curl and distend into a mocking sneer.

Brian went for another marker.

Even before Northbrook entered the bathroom, he knew something was off. The air in the hallway had been stirred. The usual stale smell and cool temperature of the hall was disrupted by the presence of another body. He squeezed his newspaper, and the ink melted under his sweaty palms. Someone had violated his sanctum. He could smell it.

He went into the bathroom and found two shoes peeping out from under the stall door.

Northbrook wanted to kick in the door, grab the kid by the collar, and throw him out on his ear. He restrained himself, however, as he had already learned the consequences of those particular actions. The large stall was still open. He could still have his peace.

He entered the second stall, lowered himself on the toilet, and stared hatefully at the feet next to him, wishing them to go away. *They mean you no harm*, Northbrook thought to himself. He turned the words into a pacifying mantra, like how the counselor instructed his group last week. Once he was moderately comfortable, Northbrook turned his attention back to his newspaper. He frowned when he saw his hands stained with purple and blue streaks of ink.

They mean you no harm.

He was relieved to discover that his opinion section was still in a decent shape. After taking out a small pair of scissors from his inside jacket pocket, he proceeded to craft another entry in his newspaper scrapbook. However, as he turned the scissors on the last corner, a distinctive chemical smell permeated his nasal cavity. Matching the smell with the squeaking sound coming from the same stall, Northbrook believed he caught himself a graffiti artist.

His lips stretched into a wicked smile.

As if sneaking up upon some small prey, Northbrook measured even his slightest movement, and tried to suppress any noise that might cause attention. He folded his newspaper slowly, and placed it on the toilet paper dispenser. Holding his belt so the buckle wouldn't clang, he stood and secured his pants. He replaced the scissors. With his ink-stained hand, he searched his pockets, and retrieved a shiny new quarter. He admired his reflection in its luster.

Northbrook steadied himself, and mentally plotted his plan of attack. After formulating various strategies for engagement, he settled on the simplest and most direct one. He would first flush the toilet. Using the discord to cover his next action, he would then glide from out of his stall, disable the other lock with the coin, and catch the hostile red-handed.

Resolute, Northbrook flushed the stall.

Brian's book bag was no different from any other at St. Pius. It was over-crowded with books, gym clothes, papers, math supplies, and a pound's worth of pens. He had pried free eight mechanical pencils, four highlighters (each of different color), two blue pens, and one red one before he found another black Sharpie. He took off the cap. The smell was nauseous.

He considered how he would go about destroying the message. Should he cover it all up (Would the marker have enough juice for that?), or should he add some other writing to discredit the accusation? He could add, "Nuh-uh!," or even possibly, "Is not! PS: You should be ashamed of yourself!" But both options seemed childish and meek.

When Brian raised the other marker, his stall door swung open. Northbrook was standing before him in his glossy shoes, flipping a coin like a 30s mobster. In an unrestrained jackal shrill, he told the young man something he already knew, that today was not Brian's lucky day.

Northbrook grabbed Brian's offending hand and yanked him out of the stall. He had it in his mind to present Brian red-handed before Father Brown. The fastest route to the principal's office was through the school's auditorium, the very room Brian feared. He may have been less concerned about his reputation if only his pants weren't knotted around his feet.

Northbrook kicked the theater's backstage door open. The loud slam of the door against the wall caught everyone's attention. For a moment, several of the students failed to realize who the prisoner was. No one assumed the hunched over figure was the kid who always sat by Paul. Yet here Brian was, flashing the student body with his pair of tighty whities.

When Katie realized who it was, she gasped. He looked so small, sad, and crumpled like a puppet with loose strings. She looked about the room for Paul, hoping he could shrug some sort of explanation, but he was nowhere to be seen.

The moment Northbrook and Brian left the room, the scandal became public. The pall of silence was pitched aside by whirlwinds of gossip.

Northbrook walked Brian across the front lobby and into the administration office. The busy crowd of secretaries, student clerks, and teachers parted to let them through. At the end of the corridor, they came upon Father Brown's office. Northbrook opened the door and hurled Brian headfirst onto Father Brown's cherry oak desk. Brian tried to cry out in pain, but no sound could be made. The wind was kicked out of him. Northbrook reclaimed Brian's wrist and waved the Sharpie-clenched hand about dramatically. Between the deafening sucks of air, as Brian tried to catch his breath, he could hear Northbrook calling for expulsion.

Father Brown wasn't interested. His attentions were focused on his new discovery of YouTube.com. He had spent the last hour viewing various clips of Donny Osmond singing "Any Dream Will Do." Justifying his lassitude, he reminded Northbrook that Brian must face the student disciplinary panel before any reprimand be enacted.

Maddened, Northbrook pushed Brian out of the building. After making sure the school doors were locked from the outside, he went back to his office. He poured himself a cup of cold coffee and brought up Brian's student record on his computer.

Mr. Northbrook took refuge in orchestrating Brian's demise.

The fall leaves crunched and shed skins of dust when the rake scraped them into a pile.

On the following Thursday, Brian spent the early afternoon raking his front yard. Left alone with his thoughts, he reviewed the events of the last week.

After he was suspended, Brian had to walk the four miles home from school. He was weary, tired, exasperated, and if the day turned any worse – he'd lose his mind. When he arrived home, his parents were waiting for him. Northbrook had called each of them at their respective practice. He stirred up their tempers to the point they canceled their appointments, cleared their books, and charged home to chastise their son.

Brian grew numb listening to them.

Northbrook told Brian's parents that he was suspended until Friday, the first date the panel could commune on the matter. Until then, they had worked up a list of chores for the young man to complete over the next four days. Among the many acts of penance, Brian would clean the garage, rake the lawn, and even paint the house. His parents threatened disownment.

They threatened to kick him out. And in response, he said nothing.

There was nothing to say.

The only person he wanted to talk to was Katie, but he had no way of contacting her. He was grounded, and his parents refused to pass along any messages. They didn't want Brian to think he was on vacation.

Paul had tried all week to get a hold of Brian. He called, emailed, faxed, Facebooked, and even sent a letter. Every attempt went unanswered. He was in the middle of ordering a Candygram when he decided to drive over. He had been hesitant to go to Brian's house, as he knew his presence could get Brian into more trouble. He didn't care; he needed to see his friend.

Weekday afternoons in Brian's suburban community were remarkably quiet. SUVs and garage doors crept along with relaxed ease. One could hear the birds pass by overhead. The sound of Paul's car radio and dragging muffler long preceded his arrival. Brian looked up from his pile of tidied leaves to see the familiar Oldsmobile approaching in the distance. He viewed the rusted jalopy with pleasure, embracing its grating noise as euphony.

Paul parked his car in the street, and told Brian to listen carefully. He said, "Denny dropped out of the class."

Brian knocked over the compost bin, and its contents were carried away by a rush of wind. He tried to stand the bin, but he was having difficulty keeping himself upright.

Paul held him up and continued. "He can't remember his dialogue. If he fails the act tomorrow, he's gonna be ineligible to play football. And that's all he's got."

"Except Katie," Brian said with lowered eyes.

"No, he doesn't."

He looked up. "What do you mean?"

"She broke up with him. After you mooned the class, Denny wouldn't stop making fun of you. She got pissed and broke up with him in front of everybody. Allenbee damn near fainted when she called him a douche-bag. It was fantastic!"

Brian wanted to rejoice, but there were still too many questions, too many problems preventing his happiness. He asked Paul about the graffiti, if she was angry, if she was okay.

"She never saw it. It was painted over less than five minutes after Northbrook grabbed you. Oh, by-the-way, we're all claiming the streaking as our senior stunt."

"If it was painted over, how do you know about it?"

"I saw it. After I saw you with Northbrook, I ran to the bathroom to see what happened." His eyes lit up. "Hey," he said excitedly, "I got a photo of it on my phone. Wanna see?"

"No."

Deflated, Paul put his phone back in his pocket.

While some of Brian's troubles were resolved, his graver fears persisted. He was still suspended, possibly soon to be expelled. His relationship with Katie was uncertain. The disciplinary interview was scheduled during first period, during the class performances. He won't get to see Katie's take on Bergman, and this regret shaped another question.

"Katie doesn't have a partner. Who is going to do the scene with her?"

Paul was pleased to see Brian pull himself out of his quicksand mind. Answering sincerely, he replied, "You are."

"But I can't."

"No one else is more due a miracle. I know these things. You are not going to be expelled. You are not going to miss our class. You are going to kiss Katie and have her babies."

"And how do you know all of this?"

"I asked my Magic 8 Ball. It's very reliable."

Paul could see Brian's eyes begin to glaze over. "Relax," Paul said. "I have a plan."

"What's that?"

"You once told me you could only do the things you want, say the things you want when you're pretending to be someone else. If you go into that room as your sweaty, nervous, inhibited, introverted self – they'll crush you. Pretend to be someone else, Brian. Be a badass."

Brian's interest was piqued.

"You're spending the night at my house."

"I can't, I'm grounded."

With a smirk, Paul replied, "Like I said, I have a

plan." He went back to his car and popped the trunk. Out of the chaos of random articles Paul used for stage props, such as a fire hydrant and a leprechaun costume; he freed the top half of a store mannequin, a ball of twine, and his resurrected boombox, mummified in duct tape. "Remember *Ferris Bueller*?"

Once the boys had converted Brian's bedroom into a makeshift stage, they went over to Paul's house, which was in a newly-developed subdivision near their school. Throughout the evening, they watched a series of classic lawyer movies and designed Brian's defense.

Before they went to sleep, Paul walked through the various elements and characteristics that went into being a badass. He showed him how to walk, talk, sit, listen, and jive.

Brian mentally envisioned himself doing all these things. It was difficult.

At 9am on Friday morning, Brian reported to the school's office wearing jeans and a t-shirt. The secretary stood from behind her desk and waved for him to follow. She took him down the hallway and into a large conference room. A massive oval-shaped table filled most of the room, and was surrounded by a ring of oversized chairs. The secretary told Brian to have a seat, as the board will be in soon. He took a chair and looked about the room. Framed prints of painted flowers lined the walls. What interested Brian the most were the honeycombs of mirrors fixed just below the ceiling's fluorescent lamp ballasts. The mirrors dispersed the light. There were no windows in the room, not a single clock.

The last detail Brian noticed was Northbrook

sitting in a folding chair in the corner. He was hunched over, examining his shoes. Not satisfied, he licked his finger and buffed out the smudge on his vamp.

The two sat alone for several minutes before the panel entered the room and took their places. Sitting directly across from him was Father Scott, whose largeness was a gross source of intimidation. His file was thicker than the others, as it contained a Sharpie in a Ziploc baggie.

While they reviewed his file, Brian went through Paul's "Seven Ways to be a Badass" speech. Rule #1 stated, "Even if you are early, act as if you are on your own time." He took a bottle of Berghoff out of his bag and set it on the table. The condensation formed a ring under the brown bottle. While his drink was a root beer, with the label facing Brian, it looked exactly like its alcoholic counterpart. The panel looked at Brian for the first time when he popped the top off on the edge of the table, and consumed half the bottle's contents with a single swallow. When they went back down to their reports, he belched.

They finished reviewing the case and Father Scott read the charges. According to Northbrook's report, Brian defaced a bathroom stall door with sexually-explicit language and "defamed" another student's reputation. The recommended course of punishment was expulsion, and the remainder of his tuition would be forfeited and donated to the school's football jersey fund.

Father Scott asked Brian if he understood the charges.

Brian ignored him and pulled out a bag of McDonald's take out, as directed by Paul's second rule,

"Break a rule they can do nothing about." Brian peeled back the wrapper to expose a steaming hot McMuffin. With a big saliva-drenched bite, he flagrantly violated Catholic law. While appearing calm and cool, Brian was having a small panic attack.

The board members all exchanged glances. A few of them even shrugged. The panel didn't know what to do, but they were willing to err on the side of punishment.

"Do you understand the charges as read by this body?" Father Scott repeated, sternly.

Brian's mouth was still full and chopping when he answered, "Yes, I do." His answer followed Rule #3: Badasses always answer honestly and to the point. He then, with his tongue, started picking food out from between his teeth.

Father Scott was confounded and exasperated at Brian's show of indifference. Not knowing exactly why he was still following protocol, he asked, "Is there anything you would like to say in your defense before we convene?"

Brian tossed his pencil at the ceiling tile above him. It stuck.

"Really, anything at all?"

"Yes, I do." As practiced, Brian stood and walked smoothly and slowly (Rule #4) around the table to the room's presentation assembly, which consisted of an overhead projector, laptop, and screen. With counted beats, he took out his flash drive, uploaded a PowerPoint file, lowered the lights to mid, and began his defense. He projected Paul's cell phone photo of the graffiti.

The panel members grunted and shook their

hands in disappointment.

"Esteemed members, this is the image I am accused of making," Brian said. "I could not help but notice there was no photo of it included in your reports. While this marking is a terrible emblem for how some of my peers view each other, in its very composition lies the proof of my innocence. Thank goodness someone decided to take a photo of it before it was painted over." He heard Northbrook humph in the back. "Let me zoom in," Brian said, and blew the image up. The words "Best Head Ever" spilled off of the screen and stretched across nearly the entire wall. The bounced light of the words lit the faces of the councilmen. "Notice the thickness of the line. How smooth the letters are drawn, almost bubbly. The penmanship is perfect."

The panel considered the craftsmanship of the writing, and a few even admired it.

Brian reset the photo's size, and advanced the slideshow. The next image was a scan of Brian's handwritten and graded essay about McCarthyism. The difference in penmanship from the prior slide prompted gasps from Brian's audience. "Here's another one. And another. Here's another." As Brian progressed through the slides, his argument was irrefutable.

He returned to the first slide and turned the lights back up in the room. Brian could see Northbrook's face turning red, and he took the teeth-mashing as a sign of encouragement.

Northbrook barked, "That doesn't prove anything. I caught you red-handed. The marker's right there!" He pointed to the Sharpie on Father Scott's case file.

Brian flashed a smile and said, "Let's take a look at

this marker, shall we?" He snatched it off the table and held it up for all to see. Remembering last night's videos, he stated, "I hereby present Evidence Example C, one fine point permanent marker. Gentlemen, this marker could not have made those graduated contour lines. The type of marker that made this line would need to have a chisel tip, like a highlighter."

Taking a risk, Brian took the Sharpie out of the bag. "This Sharpie could not make those lines, and I'm going to show you." He leaned over Father Scott, so close Brian could smell the coffee on the father's breath, and used his school record as a piece of scratch paper.

No marks were made. The Sharpie was dry. Northbrook never put the cap back on.

Brian tossed the Sharpie on the table. "It's a dead marker."

Feeling his reputation being stolen from him, Northbrook cried, "I smelled the fumes! Explain that, wise guy." Finished, he gave his tie a tug and leaned back in his hard chair.

"Gladly," Brian answered. "Let me see one of your shoes."

"What?"

"Your shoes, sir. I only need to see one."

Northbrook looked about the room, hoping for someone to end the charade. They didn't. Father Scott told him to do as the Brian had asked.

Northbrook carefully untied his right shoe and held it up for Brian. When Brian tried to take the shiny size 11, Northbrook's grip fastened, but the shoe was well oiled. It slipped out of Northbrook's hands.

Rule #5 of the Badass Doctrine: A badass turns his

enemy's pride into a weapon.

Brian wielded the Steve Madden at arms distance, and offered the board to take a whiff. While the panel was noting how the shoe polish smelled exactly like a permanent marker, Brian leaned into Father Scott's ear and whispered, "You can polish a turd…"

Father Scott chuckled. "Okay, you've proven your point. Please take your seat."

Brian sat and waited for their answer. He thought the panel would have left the room to deliberate, but they instead exchanged meaningful looks and shrugs. Father Scott nodded and noted their ruling down in Brian's case file. Once he finished his notes, he addressed Brian with folded hands. "Young man, I have a feeling you already know what I am about to say."

He didn't.

"You were caught with your pants down. Northbrook here had found graffiti, and found you with it, holding this black marker. Before I make the ruling official, I would like to ask you a question. If you were not the vandal, what would you be doing with an open marker?"

"I was declaring my love, sir. That's all."

Rule #6: Badasses are in touch with their emotions.

"Well, I appreciate your answer, though I don't quite understand it. We have seen no evidence proving that you violated any school policy. Motion for expulsion is denied; full reinstatement granted. Although I must say, there are other ways to declare your love for someone – like *telling* them. I suggest you do not hesitate. We're adjourned here."

Brian glanced over at Northbrook for confirmation. His head was in his hands, and he was rocking his body in disbelief. Brian could hear him mumble, "No-oh," in a long, protracted groan. Brian took that as a good sign.

He acted on Paul's last rule, "Badasses never outstay their welcome." He snatched his bag and sprinted out of the room.

Brian needed to find a clock. He had to get to class, but he may have been too late. As he approached the receptionist's desk, he noticed a digital clock being used as a paperweight. He read: 9:44. Allenbee's class ended in six minutes, but he had to be there in two to have enough time for his scene. If he was even a minute late, Paul had agreed to step in to save Katie's grade. But Brian didn't want Paul to step in, steal his kiss. Brian wanted to kiss her, damn it.

While the auditorium doors were the fastest way to the stage, it'd cause too much of a fuss. He was still reeling from the last time he went through those doors. When he got dressed this morning, he even took his belt in an extra notch to make sure they'd stay up throughout the day. He'd have to go in through the backstage doors at the end of south hall, a length he would normally make in three-four minutes. He'd have to run.

Paul had promised Brian to do whatever he could to stall the show. Paul looked about the backstage area, and his eyes fixed on the fog machine by stage left. He emptied the contents of the dry ice cooler into the receptacle, hoping to overfeed it, and switched the machine on. A creamy vapor pillowed out of the machine, filling the auditorium.

Brian started across the lobby and slipped. The lobby had just been mopped, and the custodian was overzealous when adding the soap to the mop water. Brian could see small soap bubbles run like water striders. He could hear the floor hiss.

In the middle of the lobby was a yellow sign. It proclaimed: Caution.

Brian started for the sign, but his feet refused to catch. By the time he made it to the marker, his clothes were covered with dark patches of citrus-scented water. He steadied himself on the plastic A-frame, and used it as a crutch until he reached the edge of the pool. The west corridor was dry, giving Brian the proper traction to let him walk. He broke into a sprint.

The theater's supply of dry ice was not abundant. The amount of fog produced was tasteful, and of great benefit to the scene in progress. Allenbee felt the fog accurately depicted the steamy pond Tom and Molly were pretending to swim in.

Paul thought about climbing the risers and dropping a sandbag on Tom's head—surely that would buy some time. But luckily for Tom, Paul discovered another way to stop the show.

He'd pull the fire alarm.

Brian made it through the labyrinth of corridors that led to the auditorium's rear entrance. There was no light inside. The painted black floor boards creaked as he advanced into the darkness. He grabbed onto the pin-rail assembly and followed the hemp lines to the back stage curtain. Having followed the fabric to its part, he moved onto to the actual stage. The front curtains were closed, but Brian could tell by the halo that lined the catwalk a scene was in progress on the apron. Laughter broke from the other side.

A sliver of light rimmed the edge of the prop door by the stack of tall flats. Brian opened the door to discover Paul upending piles of props and costumes. Paul didn't notice Brian entering the room. When he was nearly buried under the jumble, Brian asked him, "What's up?"

Paul jumped when he heard his friend's voice. He turned to him and beamed. After stumbling over piles of plastic cowboy hats, he gave Brian a tight, boisterous hug.

"Have you already gone?" Brian choked as his back popped in three places.

Paul's face slackened, and he replied flatly, "I'd rather not talk about it."

"What are you doing?"

"I was looking for a bag. Didn't want the ink to get on my hand from the fire alarm."

"You were going to pull the fire alarm?"

"I didn't know what else to do."

"Is there a fire?"

"No. Katie's up next."

"Oh. Where is she?" Brian asked. "I thought she'd be with you."

"She's in the left wing, but hold on." Paul handed him a jacket off the wardrobe rack, a tie from around his neck, and a pair of shoes he'd kicked off his own feet.

Paul undid his pants. When he handed them to

Brian, he asked, "You good?"

Brian nodded. "I think so this time."

"Good. Get Katie. Get dressed. I'll get the curtain when you're ready, all right? You've got maybe a minute. Hurry!" He pushed Brian back out on the stage.

After Brian left, Paul realized he hadn't a pair of pants for himself. He searched for a pair he could commandeer. All he could find was the bottom half of a ragged Big Bird costume.

When Brian found Katie, she was standing under a low-watt bulb, trying to make out the words on her script she had already committed to memory. He stopped for a moment and took her in. She was wearing a sensuous cocktail dress, satin evening gloves, and high heels. Her red lipstick had been recently applied, pressed, and blotted. Her hair was up in a tight French twist, which showcased the three princess-cut diamonds held in each ear. She astonished him.

Paul's pants slipped off Brian's shoulder, and the buckle clanged on the floor.

She looked up toward the noise, but did not see Brian. It was too dark.

The act on the stage ended, and Brian knew he could no longer stay hidden. He stepped into the light and let himself be shown.

Katie dropped her pages and lunged after him. She wrapped her arms around his thin frame and rocked him back and forth. She told him she missed him and asked him why he smelled like lemons.

The applause for Tom and Betty's performance had died out. The class was now waiting for the last scene to begin.

"Come on, take off your jeans." Katie cried, "We have to hurry!"

Without thinking, Brian took off his shoes and unbuttoned his pants. As he slipped them off his feet, Katie pulled his shirt off from over his head. While she was dusting off Paul's slacks, Brian could feel his opportunity start to pass. He stared at the floor. He felt chicken.

With her free hand, she touched his face. "What's darkening your brow, Mr. B.?"

He looked back up to her.

Her touch not only warmed his cheek, but also had a residual effect. She had released his heart and all of the hundreds of words it clung on to.

He tried to use his own words. "You cascade me with happiness," he said. "You are the salt of my supper. You're my Betty Ross." But they weren't good enough. So he said all he knew to say; he told her he loved her. While the words were not original, they were his own. "I love you," he said again. For the first time in his young life, he did not want to be anyone else. He wasn't nervous or scared. He was glad he was here, on this stage, with this girl, as himself.

To his surprise, she told him, in her a matter-of-fact tone, that she loved him too. Always had.

"Why didn't you say anything?" he asked.

"When I don't love you," she said, "I'll let you know."

When Brian Hughes kissed Katie Lee Marcovich, the theater curtains parted.

Chris Castle

The Mall in Rainbows

Henry Crowe walked back to the mall and fished the keys out of his pocket. He'd decided and then un-decided about ten times over. As he pulled the keys out of his pocket and jammed them in with a deep breath. He closed the door behind him without another thought.

The mall itself kept a certain amount of lights on overnight. As he stepped onto the ground floor the place was streaked in great, thick shadows; shops were visible but barely recognizable. The fast food places looked oddly beautiful and mysterious; the exclusive clothes shops seemed cheap and hokey. Henry stepped over to the fountain and dipped his fingers under the water, something that during the day he was forbidden to do. He looked down into the water and saw the coins shimmering back up at him. On his lunch break he counted them in sections; one half was tallied and one half remained.

He stepped onto the escalator and adjusted to the strange sensation of it not moving. His body wavered and he laughed, forcing one foot up and then the next, thinking; this is what it must feel like for a spaceman on the moon. The sound his feet made were not heavy and clunky as he imagined but lighter, like a football hitting a post. The sound reverberated across the whole spread of the building and as he reached the top level he was surprised to find he was out of breath. His thirties kept finding ways to keep him on his toes; sometimes it made him feel younger and other times it snapped at him and whispered he was old.

"Hey!" a voice called out from out of nowhere. Henry jolted back in shock and almost pitched back onto the escalator, grabbing the rail at the last moment. If he had had the breath he would have screamed. He looked round and saw a girl staring at him; in her left hand was a pink rucksack, in her right a can of mace.

"What are you, a thief?" the girl said coming closer. She held the mace out in front of her, like she was interviewing him.

"Not...a thief..." Henry gasped. The breathlessness mingled with the surprise and in his head he calculated if thirty seven was too young to have a heart attack.

"A pervert then," the girl continued, making it sound like twenty questions. As she drew closer he could see her eyes were tight and she looked as if she was not so much angry or scared but...peeved.

"Not a pervert...Henry Crowe," he raised his hand and waved, thinking a handshake would be out of the question.

"'Not a pervert, Henry Crowe.'" The girl's eyes slowly slipped out of a squint and she titled her head to one side, as if deciding something. "I'm Ella."

"Pleased to...meet you, Ella...please don't mace me." He pulled himself up and gripped his sides, feeling his body come back to him. As he reared up he noticed how small the girl was. Even at barely six foot he felt like a giant.

"So what's the story, are you breaking in or

something?" she took a step back and jammed the mace into her bag. Henry noticed she left it sticking out though, just in case.

"I just wanted to come and see it without all the people, I guess," Henry folded his arms, feeling more foolish than unnerved. It was part of the truth, which is a lot more than most offer up to a stranger, he thought. She 'uh-huh'-ed in reply, unconvinced. Great, he thought, I've met the last genuinely perceptive teenager left in the country.

"You're the security guard from the daytime, aren't you?" She scooped the bag onto her back. He had the idea she'd known that from the start but just wanted it confirmed.

"That's right. And you work here, but I couldn't say which shop you're in. I'd say it was on this floor though." Henry recognized her from one of the places; she'd seemed sharp, too smart for her uniform and slightly detached from the rest of the kids. Like a teenager who smoked but knew it was dumb and something she'd drop when it came to living in the real world.

"I work in the coffee slash food establishment. We provide both beverages and burgers made to your every need." She was smirking but there was a trace of a blush from when he'd mentioned the correct floor. He smiled.

"I hear it's a good one," he said and looked around to find it, just to the left of where they were standing.

"You want to grab a coffee? I can't start up the grill but I could set up that much. I figure you can't bust me, seeing as how I could bust you." She shrugged and almost smiled.

"Like Butch and Sundance," he said and smiled.

Her face was a complete blank and he felt his heart sink a little. Thanks, thirty-seven. "Forget-"

"Kidding," she broke in and smiled. "What, you thought I would only watch 'Fast and Furious?'" She looked round and he returned the blank expression. "You are kidding, right?"

"Yeah...sure. Well, I brought a flask, but maybe we could share it out. I got food too." He felt ridiculous as they began walking, looking at her pink rucksack, but alive too. Take that, thirty seven, he thought and smiled.

"So, are we going to get the whole 'why we're here stuff' out of the way early or late?" she said, as she slipped behind the counter. Henry watched her as she moved around the counter, flipping the cups and flicking switches. She caught him looking and raised an eyebrow.

"I thought teenagers were supposed to be awkward and clumsy. You're moving like a skater behind there," he said, pointing to a table. She nodded.

"'Teenager?' I'm nineteen, for Christ-sakes." She shook her head and filled up the first cup.

"My mistake; you're ancient." He said, as he began to lift out the stuff he'd packed into his own satchel. As he put them on the table, he glanced out to the rest of the mall; from the bright light of the café, the place looked incredibly dark, as if they were the last two people on earth.

"Thinking like we're the survivors in a zombie flick, huh?" she said as she put the cup in-front of him. She set down a napkin and smiled again, knowing she had read his mind. He shook his head.

"This is a latte, half twist, with a jolt of lemon." She said, looking down to the Styrofoam cup.

"It sure is," he said looking it over, half expecting an actual lemon to bob up to the surface. When it didn't, he decided to risk it. He sipped it once and looked over to her. "That's not bad. Not bad at all."

"It's my favorite. The trick is to judge the measure of lemon right. If the guy's a jerk he gets too much. If he's okay, I stop the second serving a little early to get it just right." She walked away to grab her own drink. Henry looked at her, then down to his drink and was pretty sure she'd just paid him a compliment.

"So what have you got?" he said as she sat down. Her cup was smaller and she tilted it, to show there was nothing in it.

"May I?" she asked, pointing to the flask.

"You may, but I don't think it'll be half as good as what you've got going on here, to be honest." He unscrewed the cap and looked to her cup. She rolled her eyebrows but let him pour.

"Thank you. I want to see if you're coffee's good enough to justify never coming in here and ordering." She sipped it and nodded her head. He could tell it wasn't half as good but she was trying to be polite. "So, why don't you come in here?" she said and he laughed; it was the roundabout insult that only a kid could pull off without sounding mean.

"I don't come in here because it's busy," he said and took another gulp. He could feel her eyes on him. "You're squinting at me again, I can feel it."

"It's because you're not telling me the whole truth again." She drank from her cup again, almost absent-mindedly, still looking at him.

"I never know what to order from the board," he

sighed and looked over to the blackboard. "I mean, I don't know what the hell half of it means." He felt himself blush. He was actually blushing over this. Henry shook his head. "Anyway," he said, desperate to change the subject.

"Anyway," she repeated, still smiling. Suddenly her face hardened. "So, I broke up with my boyfriend and I can't crash at my friend's until the weekend so I'm sleeping here." She leant back, still looking at him, waiting for his reaction. "You wanted to change the subject."

"I was thinking more about tea," Henry said, seeing how relieved, embarrassed and angry she was all at the same time. So many emotions, so few years, his dad used to say. "That makes sense, I mean...hotels are expensive, I guess." he smiled and wondered if he'd ever offered a lamer answer. "You were living together for a long time?"

"Not really. He decided to go back to his wife in the end," she let the last words hang in the air. "Does that shock you?" Henry looked at her and saw her for what she was then, a mess of emotions, all tangled up and coming apart.

"No, not really," he said, surprised at how good it felt to be totally honest. She made to speak and then swallowed, taken aback. Her face stayed hard but somehow softened too, around the edges of her eyes, the corners of her mouth. Henry realized she was adjusting to the idea that someone was prepared to tell her the truth.

"Good. I wish you could have met him, just to tell me he was a dick from the outset," she said and leant over, pouring some of his coffee into her cup. Some of the foam spilled over onto the table and they both reached for the napkin; Henry beat her to it.

"I wish I could have, too" he said, carefully wiping around the pooled ring between them.

"So you're going to stay for two more nights?"

"That's right. I got my sleeping bag and the key to the fire escape. The others come in here at weekends some times when they get back from parties. It's okay here, you know?"

"As long as you're not on the street, I guess," he said, taking another draw from his cup. He offered her some more, but she shook her head.

"Henry Crowe, you are by far and away the worst security guard I have ever met," she lifted her cup in a toast and he brushed his against hers.

"Thank you, Ella. That means a lot," he said. She sat back and slowly tilted her head back. He did the same, not understanding. A shot ran through him; "Is someone coming?"

"Come on, it's about time, don't you think?" she said, still nodding back to the counter. Another bolt ran through Henry of an entirely different kind, but still just as queasy. "Ella, I-"

"It's the perfect time to read the board, Henry. No-one's around, right?" She slid out of the booth and walked away, already looking up to the menu.

"Right," Henry said, trying to slide out as briskly as she had done, but got jammed up on the way, so the cool 'swoosh' noise she had so perfectly made as she left sounded more like the tired squeak of an old man's fart.

"Okay, so are you going to tell me why you came here?" They'd stepped out onto the concourse and were looking out to the mall from the top deck. "Apart from 'there are no people,'" she added in a gruff voice.

"Man, that sounds just like me," he said looking round to her.

"Come on, I told you mine, you have to tell me yours," she took a bite out of the apple he'd thrown to her and the crunching noise echoed like a gunshot. "Wow. That carried," she said, looking down to the fruit, like she didn't quite recognize it anymore.

"Yeah, you told me but you didn't tell me everything," he said and watched as she very deliberately looked back out to the shops. He wasn't sure if he'd hit a nerve and was sure he didn't want to upset her. What the hell, he thought.

"I came back because I used to come here with an old girlfriend." Now he had said it out loud, he realized just how small it sounded. It was his turn to look out to the shops, even as she turned round to face him. "We used to know the guard and he'd let us in here on Sundays when it was closed."

"Shops closed on Sundays?" she said, her voice genuinely stunned. She sounded like someone had just run over her dog. Oh man.

"That's what's shocking you the most? Seriously?" He shook his head and folded his arms across his chest.

"Sorry," she said and walked back a step to set the apple down on the bench behind them. "So, was she the one then? I don't know... your true love or something?" He waited for her to return to the railing, thinking she clearly *did* know more than... or something.

"So anyway, we used to come here and I thought

I'd come back, just once, to see what it was like." He looked out and saw the stars were slotting into place above them.

"So I guess I rained on your parade, huh?" she poured two more coffees from his newly refilled flask and handed one over to him.

"Thanks. Not really, I knew as soon as I stepped in, I knew it was kind of stupid." He blew the steam away and drank. "Dumb, huh?"

"Not really," she said. "I think you can meet the right person at the wrong time." She frowned as she drank and Henry quietly marveled at how she'd off-handed just summed up everything he was feeling right then.

"I think that's probably what I was trying to say," he said quietly. "Wise words." For a long moment they stood in silence, the night sky highlighting the windows of some shops, while leaving others in complete darkness.

"I had a boyfriend before the married guy and I left him because he was too good to me. He used to paint my toes and make me laugh." She looked over to him. "I don't think I'm wise at all, not really."

Henry looked over to her and saw she was trying not to cry now. It was the last two words, 'not really' that made it sound so true to him. It's all the real words people stop themselves from saying as they get older, he thought.

"So, are you lonely now?" she asked. Her voice was small now, but it still carried perfectly in the empty building. She was asking him but he got the idea they both needed to hear the answer.

"Sometimes, when I think about it, I feel lonely.

Sometimes I feel sad. So I try not to think about it too much." It was what he felt and he had said it exactly. Even though it was a sad thing to say, a part of him felt his heart soar, just to tell the truth and do it honestly.

"That's sad," she said.

"But it's not the worst thing," he added and somehow they agreed on that.

"So why are you working here?" she called out from the bottom of the escalator and started walking.

"I am working here because it is close and is for the summer," Henry shouted back as he walked down the frozen steps. "I am going back to work as a teacher in September." He reached the middle of the steps and met her there.

"Why are you working here?" he called out, realizing he didn't have to shout at that meeting in the middle point, making them both laugh.

"I am working here because I need the money," she said. Henry could tell she had turned round and was walking backwards up the steps. He awkwardly did the same going down, so they were facing each other as they got further apart.

"I am also working here because I am lazy and am not motivated to do anything else." She reached the top step and raised her hands, as if she'd scaled a mountain. He copied her and they both gripped their hips and took a loud breather. "Two minutes," she gasped. Henry met the statement with a thumbs up.

"I think I can only do this one more time," she called down.

"Okay...I'm old, what's you're excuse?" he cupped

his hands to call up and noticed his voice changed slightly, making him smile.

"My generation's lazy," she called down and cleared her throat.

"That's not an answer," he shouted up, throwing her off. She opened her arms up in exasperation. "Sorry." She cleared her throat for a second time.

"Why don't we quit?" she hollered and began walking.

"I will quit in exactly two weeks, when I've made my money and been to my nephew's birthday party." Henry stomped towards the middle, sucking up his breath and repeating the question.

As they reached the center, she rolled her finger in a circle and slumped down onto the step. Henry acted disappointed but gladly sat down on his side. While they took turns in panting, he carefully poured out the coffee and leant over to hand her a cup. He was surprised at how light the canister was; only about two cups left in it, he guessed. Somehow, the idea of that made him feel sad. Henry looked up to the glass ceiling and saw the moon was full in the sky and realized it would soon be morning.

"I take the photos from the junk lab," she said quietly, as she set the cup down on the step.

"What's the junk lab?" he asked, silently praying to Christ it wasn't anything like a meth lab.

"It's where they throw away all the old photos that no-one collects from the lab. They have a window of three months and then they toss them. They're supposed to securely dispose of them but no-one cares. I collect them, like I'm doing them a big favor and take them with me. The guys don't ask questions, they just stare at my ass as I walk away." She ran her hand through her hair and that action, coupled with the dirty filter of the glass suddenly made her look very old, as if she had already lived most of her life.

"What are in the photos?" he asked.

"Mostly nothing; just stupid everyday things. I don't keep hardly any of them. I always shred them before I throw them away, though, so they stay private. Apart from me, I guess." She described a few of the pictures and Henry watched as she locked her hands together. For a second she looked as if she were praying and then it was as if she'd sensed that too, unlocking them suddenly and setting them down on her knees.

"But..." Henry said quietly, almost whispering. There was more to it, he thought, in the spaces between the words, in the pauses between the details.

"I wonder why they didn't collect them, you know? If they just forgot or if they moved suddenly; or if something terrible happened to make them forget about the small things, the little duties like finding a ticket and collecting some dumb holiday snaps." For a second there was silence but Henry knew somehow not to speak. "Does that sound stupid?"

"No, it doesn't sound stupid," he said. Her voice was quiet when she asked the question and for the first time that night, she sounded young, impossibly young and scared like other kids.

"Then how does it sound?" she asked. Henry knew she wanted to hear more and she knew he wanted to say more.

"It sounds beautiful," he said quietly. Henry watched as she rested her head against the glass and looked up to the ceiling full of stars. He did the same, mirroring the same soft thud as his head pushed against the side.

"Good," she whispered.

The time drifted away in idle talk. The two of them stood in-front of shop windows, picking out their clothes; sometimes they mentioned regular customers and their odd habits, which made them both laugh. Henry noticed they both winced as the place grew steadily lighter; the night was drifting away and the pre-dawn grey was bringing everything into view. It made the place look suddenly mechanical and a little ugly too. He knew Ella felt the same way.

"It doesn't feel the same, window shopping without the shadows," she said and he understood what she meant. "I feel like a vampire," she said but her smile was sad.

"Come on," he said, nodding over to the fountain. "There's one last thing before we go." Henry reached into his bag and unzipped a compartment.

"If you've got some pot, I am both shocked and extremely pleased," she said, her eyes suddenly lighting up. Until then, he hadn't realized how tired she'd looked in the last hour or so. My god, he thought, she's not used to staying up all night. He suppressed a smile and hooked out the pile of sunglasses; all wrapped up together in a bundle with elastic bands. He led her over to the fountain.

"Now, if I can just get this right," Henry said, feeling his heart speed up as he tried to remember how he'd set it up all that time ago. Without a word, he began climbing the fountain, glad he'd remembered to wear his hiking boots for grip.

"What the hell, Henry?" she said, her voice halfway between shock and a fit of giggles. He reached the top and set the sunglasses one on top of the other, in a high, mazy stack. When he was done, he swung back a little to make sure they were tilted at the right angle. Maybe, maybe not, he thought. He looked up and saw the grey clouds were starting to come apart in the sky. Too late now, Henry muttered to himself and clambered back down.

"Just watch," he said as he jumped the last few feet over the rim of the fountain. Henry stood by the side of her and looked up as the sun broke through. "Wait for it, wait for it..."

The sun broke through and the beams of light hit the colored lenses. It happened just how he'd remembered it; the prisms of light ran through the glasses. They reflected on the water and filtered back to the ceiling. Rainbows were everywhere; on the water, on the ceiling, running through the corners of the mall. All in one clear streak of light, bouncing to a half dozen places. All lit by the dawn light and just how he remembered it.

"That...is the coolest thing I've ever seen," she whispered by his side. Henry looked over and saw her mouth had actually fallen open.

"Cooler than 'Fast and the Furious'?" He asked as the beams grew stronger.

"Hell yeah," she whispered, following the colors all the way to the top.

Henry followed her out the fire escape and out into the streets. It was barely six but already people were starting to drift onto the streets. A few shutters rattled in the distance and the newspapers were already in their containers on the corner. Henry winced, disorientated by the sudden openness of the town. He looked over and saw Ella was doing the same.

"Okay then," he said. Nearby a café was already open but he knew they wouldn't go for breakfast.

"Okay then," she said, looking back at him as she stretched. Before she could say anything else, he handed her the set of glasses.

"For another time," he said and smiled. She took them and lifted them up to him, like they were a prize. Henry edged back and she did too. Without another word she started walking down the street, adjusting the strap of her backpack as she went. The sun was already high in the sky and it was going to be a hot day. Henry watched her until she reached the corner of the street. She looked back and waved once. He did the same and then she was gone. Henry turned and walked down the street, stopping to buy a paper, feeling more tired and more alive than he had felt in a very long time.

Made in the USA
Charleston, SC
16 May 2012